ABOUT THE AUTHOR

Kate Hoffmann has written over
Her first book was published in
brated twenty years as a roman
Kate's interests include theate
design and vegetarian cooking.
Wisconsin with her cat, Chloe, and many small dust bunnies.

Books by Kate Hoffmann

Prologue

THE WIND HOWLED outside the house on Gordon Road, shaking the windows. The dream had Ryan Quinn in its grip, and though he wanted to wake up, he felt as if the darkness had swallowed him whole.

In the dream, a knock sounded at the bedroom door, so loud that it shook the floor. He slowly crossed the room, the floor icy cold against his bare feet. He stopped short as the knob began to turn, the terror welling up inside of him. The door swung open and a huge figure filled the space.

Ryan's breath came in shallow gasps as the fear overwhelmed him. He looked up from the man's boots to his cold weather gear. The hood of the man's jacket was pulled low over his face and Ryan watched as he brushed the hood back.

A scream tore from Ryan's throat and he bolted up in his bed, his heart slamming against his chest. His twin brother, Rogan, pushed up from his pillow on the bed next to him, rubbing his eyes. "Jaysus, Ryan, wake up. You're having a nightmare."

Ryan swallowed hard, pulling the blankets up to his chin. "I'm okay. I'm okay."

Rogan shook his head. "What was it this time?"

Since their father's death a year ago, Ryan had had trouble sleeping. He'd been plagued with vague, unsettling dreams, dreams that reflected the grief and fear that existed in the Quinn house. But this was a new one, more vivid and frightening.

Ryan shivered, his body trembling uncontrollably. "It—it was Dad."

Rogan crawled out of his bed and sat down on the edge of Ryan's mattress. "Really. You saw him in your dream?"

Ryan nodded, swallowing back the fear. Tears filled his eyes and he brushed one off his cheek. "He was frozen. His face was made of ice and his eyes were black holes. And there was snow in his hair and beard."

"Did he say anything?"

"No. But he smiled at me."

"It was just a dream," Rogan said.

Ryan turned to him. "Some nights, before I go to sleep, I imagine that he's still alive. I imagine that he walked off the mountain and is living somewhere in Nepal or Tibet. That he's safe."

"He isn't," Rogan said. "Mum says that he's dead and we need to accept that. But…sometimes I wish he was alive, too."

"Do you think they'll ever find him?"

"Mal says that even if they do, they could never bring him home. It would be impossible."

"I wish I could see him just once more. Just so I could remember him."

"What would you say to him?" Rogan asked.

Ryan had to consider his answer. He knew he shouldn't be angry with his father, but there was a tiny part of him that was. Max Quinn had promised to always come back, but he'd broken his promise, turning Ryan's world upside down.

Their lives had changed overnight. Money was suddenly in very short supply, and the worry over the family finances was deeply etched in their mother's face. They'd had to leave their little house in Rotorua, leave their friends and school and come to live in Raglan with their mother's parents.

Lydie Quinn had been sad for nearly a year, staying in her room and not coming out, even for Ryan and his three siblings. Ryan had been afraid for such a long time, and he wasn't sure how to help his mother. But he'd found odd jobs and made a few dollars here and there, each week handing over the money to his grandmother for groceries.

And though his siblings still worshipped the man who had been their father, Ryan was the only one who also saw that he'd had flaws. He'd left his family with nothing. He'd thought he was invincible—and he'd been wrong.

Rogan pulled the blanket up and crawled into the bed. Ryan moved over to make room. "Mum wants to drive to Rotorua tomorrow so we can go to the cemetery. It's been a year. They put up a monument and she wants us to see it."

"Is it going to be sad? I don't want to watch her cry anymore."

"I expect it will be," Rogan said. "But best to keep our chins up and carry on."

Ryan flopped back on the pillow, his gaze fixed on the shadows that danced on the ceiling. "I want him to come home."

"I know," Rogan said, lying down beside him. "Someday, maybe we can go look for him. We could bring him home and put him in the cemetery."

Ryan shook his head, the thought of seeing his father frozen in time more frightening than the nightmare. "I don't want to remember him that way. I want to remember him like he was when he was alive." Before he'd broken his promise and died.

"Maybe you're right," Rogan said.

"But I do want to climb mountains someday," he said. "Just like Dad. I want to see all the things that he saw."

"We will," Rogan said.

Ryan closed his eyes and tried to picture his father alive and happy. But no matter how hard he tried, the image of the man in the dream kept nagging at his brain. How could this have happened to Max Quinn? He'd always told his children that he would keep himself safe, that they had nothing to fear.

Had he forgotten his promise? Or maybe promises didn't mean anything to grown-ups. Well, it would mean something to him. Ryan made a silent vow—he would never break a promise, ever.

"Go to sleep," Rogan said. "You'll feel better in the

morning." Rogan put his arm around his brother, and Ryan clutched him tightly.

"Promise me that you'll never die," Ryan whispered.

"I won't. I promise. Now you promise, too."

"I won't die. Not until I'm an old man. I promise."

_1_

RYAN QUINN STARED out the rain-blurred windscreen of Rogan's Land Rover, his gaze fixed on the dark tarmac. In the distance, the landing beacons from Auckland's airport illuminated the night sky.

"How long are you going to wait?"

"All night if I have to," Ryan murmured, glancing over at his twin brother, slumped in the driver's seat. "They're coming in from Los Angeles on a private jet. I don't reckon they'll be keeping to a strict schedule."

"Serena Hightower," Rogan said, shaking his head. "How did you get so lucky?"

Ryan shrugged. "I'm not sure I'd call it lucky. It's just another job."

"Yeah, but the scenery is going to be splendid," Rogan said, reaching for the coffee he'd set in the cup holder. "What are you going to do with them? I asked Dana what your plans were, but she said they're top secret."

"We're going to Fiji."

"Really? We've never guided in Fiji before. That's more of a vacation spot."

"We'll do some light trekking, maybe some climbing. Surfing. Sailing."

"What about supplies and equipment and—"

"It's not that kind of trip. I'm just on board as…an advisor. Someone who can take care of all the details for whatever they want to do."

"Kind of like a…babysitter?"

Ryan glanced over at his brother, ready with a retort. But there was no way around it. That was pretty much the job description. But how the hell was he supposed to refuse the offer? He was getting his regular rate plus expenses *and* a promised bonus at the end, all of which he intended to keep for himself. And if he did the job well, there might be other opportunities—which meant a chance to carve out a life of his own, away from the family business. "I prefer to call it a facilitator."

He'd been considering a break from the family adventure-guiding business for a long time, and lately, it seemed as if that time was now. Both Mal and Rogan were settling down with women they'd met, planning their futures, searching for ways to cut back on the trips they took for Max Adrenaline. They'd both assumed that Ryan would happily take over the brunt of the work.

But he'd made no promises to them and had plans of his own—he wanted to start a surf school. He lived right on the beach; he'd been surfer since the age of nine. And he'd always been a decent teacher. The only thing he didn't have was the money to make it happen.

His fee, plus a big tip on this job would provide a good start.

"How did you get this job?" Rogan asked.

"I guided a bloke named Thom Perry last year. He was on our Mount Blanc trip. Perry owns Greenmoor Studios in Los Angeles. Serena Hightower is starring in some big blockbuster they have coming out after Christmas. She's marrying her boyfriend right before the premiere, and he doesn't want any bad press."

"Bad press?"

"This is her hen party. She and her bridesmaids want one last fling before she gets married, and Perry wants to make sure they don't create any problems for the studio."

"So it's your job to get her safely to the altar so this bloke's movie can make more millions?"

"That's about it," Ryan said. "How hard can it be? Five women on a tropical island."

"So, will you be hiring the male stripper or are you providing those services yourself?"

"It's not like that," he said. "Ms. Hightower wants an adventure. According to her instructions, she doesn't want to spend every minute working on her tan. I expect we won't be sipping mimosas by the pool the entire time."

"So you'll be doing a lot of shopping?"

"Definitely not on the itinerary. Perry has a man in Fiji who will help me with the arrangements. Arthur Cawaru. He'll meet up with me there."

"We're splitting the fee with him?"

Ryan shook his head. "Nope. Like I said, the studio

is paying all the bills. And this isn't a Max Adrenaline job. I'm freelancing on this."

"Wow," Rogan muttered. "Mal isn't going to like that."

"This isn't a guiding job. I'm not using company equipment or money. And I don't care what the hell Mal does and doesn't like these days," Ryan muttered. "He's been so caught up in planning the Everest trip that he's not interested in anything else."

Max Quinn, their father, had died nearly twenty years before while guiding a group of climbers to the summit of Everest. Before his death, he'd parlayed his considerable fame as a mountaineer into an adventure business with his Aussie friend and business partner, Roger Innis—who had taken total control of the company, and its profits, after Max's accident.

And now, with the recent discovery of their father's body on Everest, there had been a push for his three adventuring sons to make a pilgrimage of sorts to Max Quinn's final resting place, to retrieve his effects and bury him properly. Mal, Ryan's older brother, was all for the trip, along with publishing a biography that he and his fiancée, Amy Engalls, were writing about his father.

But not everyone was so enthusiastic about their expedition to Everest. Roger Innis was mounting an expedition of his own to recover their father's effects, including his climbing journal, which Innis considered company, not personal, property. Mal suspected that Innis was afraid he might be blamed for the mistakes made that day. And Ryan and Rogan knew there were other secrets that might be exposed if their father's journal got into the wrong hands. The secrets in that book could shatter their perfect memory of their father —and destroy the family he'd left behind.

Ryan drew a deep breath. "We need to tell Mal about Dad and the Montgomery woman. He can still call an end to this."

"There's no stopping him," Rogan said. "The trip is a go." He paused. "And I'm going with him. I'm not going to let Roger Innis use his expedition to make himself look like the hero."

"But you said it was morbid."

"Yeah," Rogan said. "But I've had a change of heart. Claudia has pointed out that I can't really get on with my future until I deal with my past. Maybe this trip is what it will take for me to understand who he was. And who I am."

"You know who he was," Ryan countered. "He was our father. A philanderer."

"That's not all he was. Listen, someday I'm going to be a father. And I won't have Dad around to talk to about it. So I'd like to know him a little better. And I want the truth of why he died on that mountain."

"And what if the journal's not there? What if he just died there on the mountain, without anything important to say to his family? Or what if he mentions that Montgomery woman? How do you think that will make Mum feel?"

Rogan drew a deep breath. "I don't know. But it's time we found out."

"You and Mal can go right ahead."

"It's something we should all do together," Rogan insisted.

"Count me out. I'm happy with what I know. I don't see the need to stir it all up again. It almost destroyed us once already." Ryan's chest tightened and he swallowed back a wave of emotion.

His family had never really dealt with his father's death. At the time, Ryan's mother, Lydie Quinn, had been so emotionally fragile herself that she hadn't been able to help her children through the tragedy. Ryan had stood by helplessly as all the happiness had drained out of their lives.

Along the way, Ryan had learned to control his emotions, to stop caring about anything that might make him happy. He'd lived his life waiting for the next disaster to befall their family and building a high wall around his heart to protect himself from the pain.

Malcolm and Rogan had found happiness. They'd fallen in love and were looking forward to rosy futures. But Ryan would never allow himself to be that vulnerable. He couldn't bring himself to trust that deeply.

"You're going to have to make a decision soon," Rogan said. "We leave in three months."

"Have a good trip," he muttered.

An uneasy silence fell over the interior of the Range Rover. As if he didn't already feel like an outsider in his own family, this didn't make things much better. He and his brothers had always agreed on most subjects, but since Amy and Claudia had come into the picture, that had all changed.

"Is that your plane?" Rogan asked.

Ryan looked up and saw a small jet appear out of the darkness. It rolled to a stop about twenty meters from the car.

"Jaysus, you *will* be traveling in style," Rogan said, laughing softly.

"Thanks for the lift," Ryan said. "I'll see you in a week."

The door to the plane dropped down, and Ryan jumped out and grabbed his gear from the rear seat. "Wish me luck," he said.

"I don't think you'll be needing any," Rogan said. "Stay out of trouble."

Ryan waved and swung his bag over his shoulder, then jogged across the tarmac to the waiting plane. A young man appeared in the doorway as Ryan climbed the steps.

"Mr. Quinn?"

"Yes," Ryan said.

"Welcome aboard. I'm Miles DuMont. I'm the studio publicist. It's a pleasure to meet you."

Ryan shook his hand. "A publicist?"

"Oh, don't worry," he whispered. "You'll barely know I'm here. I'm just along to make sure we control the message. And get a few good photos."

"The message? What does that mean?" Ryan asked as he moved past him.

"Ms. Hightower tends to find herself in the middle of a media firestorm wherever she goes. I'm the one who carries the fire extinguisher."

The interior of the plane was dark and silent. Ryan stowed his gear in a locker and glanced toward the back of the plane. "They've all had plenty to drink," Miles said. "Come on back. I'll introduce you to Serena."

Ryan followed Miles down the aisle of the plane. Four passengers were curled up in the wide leather seats, sound asleep, but a reading light glowed from a seat at the rear.

"Ms. Hightower?"

Ryan held his breath when he got his first glimpse of the actress. She was stunning. Her long hair was pulled back from her fresh-scrubbed face, and she wore dark-rimmed glasses, which did nothing to hide her large liquid-blue eyes.

"Ms. Hightower, this is Ryan Quinn, the guide."

She smiled warmly and Ryan's pulse leaped. He knew he ought to say something, but he couldn't seem to put the words together. Hell, he was the last guy in the world who would be starstruck, but she was possibly the most beautiful woman he'd ever met. "Hello," he finally managed.

"Hi," she said, sending him a coy smile. She stared at him for a long moment and Ryan wondered if she could read his thoughts. Not that his thoughts were any different from those of every other bloke who had the pleasure of meeting her. She slowly reached out her hand, and Ryan took it.

"I—I have some interesting adventures planned for you," he said, his fingers tingling.

"Good. I'm looking forward to having some fun. Do you like to have fun, Quinn? Or are you like Thom Perry? Do you think I need to behave myself?"

"I—" Ryan frowned, drawing his hand away. She

spoke with a distinct British accent. He'd assumed she was American, but clearly he'd been wrong. "What was the question?"

She laughed softly. "Miles, why don't you get Quinn something to eat and drink. We've got a long flight ahead of us and I'm sure he'd like to settle in."

"Yes, Ms. Hightower."

With that, Ryan nodded, then turned and made his way to a seat at the front of the plane. He looked back once to see Serena leaning into the aisle and watching his retreat.

"Be warned," Miles said. "That innocent smile hides a very naughty side. Don't be taken in."

"No, of course not," Ryan murmured.

But as he sank into the soft leather seat, a strange sense of anticipation settled over him. He couldn't help but be curious. Who was Serena Hightower? And why did the simple touch of her hand startle him so?

He rubbed his hand on the faded fabric of his jeans, as if the action might banish all thoughts of Serena from his head. But it didn't work. Unless he regained a measure of control, this was going to be a very long trip.

SERENA HIGHTOWER STARED out the window of the jet, her gaze fixed on the blinking light at the end of the wing. She closed her eyes and drew a deep breath, trying to clear the chaotic thoughts from her mind.

She rubbed her hands together, wondering why the effects of the man's touch seemed to linger. Yes, Ryan Quinn was attractive...and sexy...and he had a dangerous air. And, yes, any woman would find him irresistible. But she was engaged. Engaged to be married in a few weeks! And all she could think about was some stranger she'd just met.

"Ryan," she murmured. "Ryan Quinn."

Serena groaned. How had she allowed this engagement to get so far? When she'd accepted Ben's proposal, she'd never really believed it would result in a wedding. She'd been infatuated, giddy with the romance of being in love. But the realities of their situation had soon begun to emerge. They hadn't dated very long, and Serena had soon realized that she didn't really know Ben. Though they were both actors with high-profile careers and permanent places in the gossip magazines, they had very different ideas about a commited relationship, especially when it came to fidelity.

Serena had spent a lifetime watching her parents make a hash of their multiple marriages. Living life as the only child of a celebrity couple should have opened her eyes to the realities of love, especially the fact that actors had so many temptations to stray.

When they'd first gotten involved, Serena hadn't cared that Ben Thayer had a reputation as a player— she'd just taken it as a reality of the biz. Besides, she hadn't been concerned about getting hurt, because she was going into the marriage with her eyes wide open.

So how had she lost control of this?

For some reason she'd assumed that the media would be happy to report the engagement and then move on to more interesting stories. But they'd immediately pressed her to set a wedding date. She'd just tossed a date out, figuring she could always change her mind. Unfortunately, her "team" had taken the date as gospel and had begun to plan, clearing her schedule, searching for wedding venues, hiring a wedding planner.

While she'd been away shooting a movie, her entire wedding had been planned for her, and she'd passed the point of no return before she'd even had a chance to scream "Stop!" Breaking her engagement now would bring a riot of bad press at a time when her career and her reputation as an actress hung in the balance.

Serena had always wanted to be taken seriously as an actress. Yet most of her career to date had been built on popular and not critically acclaimed films. But her most recent film was different. It was her chance to show she was a capable actress.

She would no longer be the child of Will Sheridan and Cassandra Hightower-Fellowes, or the fiancée of Ben Thayer, or the beautiful face that graced the pages of fashion magazines. She wouldn't be famous for being famous. Once this movie was released, she'd be Serena Hightower, a serious actress.

And then she'd finally be satisfied, finally be happy with her life. This had to be it. She'd tried everything else—meditation, yoga, Kabbalah, juicing—whatever trend had come along, Serena had tried it, hoping that she'd find the answers to her questions. One question, actually. With everything she'd achieved in life, everything she possessed, why couldn't she be happy?

It was a simple question, yet one that seemed to plague her mind. There had to be something more to life than this. She had money. She had fame. She had every possession she could ever wish for. And if she went ahead with the wedding, she'd have a marriage.

Serena reached out and poured herself a glass of warm champagne. They'd opened the bottles hours ago as a celebration of the adventure they were about to have. But now, the taste of the flat champagne mirrored her feelings.

She pushed out of her seat and wandered to the front of the jet. Her four bridesmaids were sound asleep, exhausted from the excitement of the trip and too much champagne. Miles had his nose buried in his laptop. She glanced over at the passenger they'd taken aboard in Auckland.

Serena plopped down beside him. "Can't sleep?"

He turned away from the window and met her gaze. "I never sleep on planes."

The urge to touch him again was overwhelming. She wanted to reach out and run her fingers through his thick dark hair. Why did she find him so fascinating? She'd known her share of handsome men. But Ryan Quinn wore his good looks like he wore his clothes, casually and comfortably. This was a man who never worried over wrinkles and Botox and the effect aging would have on his career. This was a real man.

"So, you're the nanny Thom has sent along to watch over us," Serena said, settling back into the leather seat and tucking her feet up under her.

"Nanny?"

"What do you prefer to be called?" she asked.

"Quinn," he said. "You can call me Quinn."

She fixed him with her most charming gaze. "What

did he tell you, Quinn? Are you meant to keep us out of trouble?"

"I'm supposed to facilitate your travel and activities," he said.

"If that's your story," she said with a shrug. "But you don't have to pretend. I know why he sent you. He wants to make sure I'm safely delivered to the altar after Christmas."

"Is that expected to be a problem?"

Serena sighed. "No. Of course not. I'm ready to get married."

And yet even when she said the words out loud, Serena couldn't make herself finish the thought—ready to get married *to Ben*. Was she really ready to marry him? Was she even in love with him? If she was, why was she trying to tease this handsome stranger into conversation when she ought to just go back to her seat and sleep?

"How did you get talked into taking this job?" she asked.

"I guided Thom on a climbing trip last year. He thought I was the right man for the job."

She laughed softly. "I can imagine," Serena murmured. Thom was a crafty sort, she mused. He could have sent some gruff, middle-aged security sort, but instead, he'd sent someone young and hot, the kind that her four single bridesmaids would find irresistible. "You're going to be the hit of the party."

Serena reached out and grabbed his glass from the table in front of him, draining the last bit of whiskey and water from the bottom. "I'll get you another," she said.

"I'm fine," Ryan replied.

"I'm not," Serena said.

She crawled out of her seat and made her way to the small galley near the cockpit door. After she filled two tumblers with ice, she grabbed the whiskey bottle and returned to her seat next to Ryan.

"So, why don't you tell me all about yourself," Serena said, pouring him a glass.

He pointed to the whiskey, filled to the brim. "Are you trying to get me pissed?"

"It's a long flight. We have a lot of time to kill. And I'll get bored if you don't tell me some interesting stories. I'm just getting you relaxed."

"I'm always relaxed," he said.

"Lucky you," she said. "I never am."

He pushed the glass in her direction. "Why don't you drink it, then?"

She'd already had too much champagne and was beginning to feel the effects of a hangover. But she picked up the glass and took a sip, then set it down. Serena's gaze met his, and for a long moment, she couldn't look away. Would she be so attracted to him if she loved Ben? Her heart said no, but there was so much riding on this wedding now, she had to be sure. Letting her impulsive nature take over, she leaned forward and kissed him.

It wasn't a passionate kiss. Nor was it platonic. It existed in the strange space in between. She drew back, her face warming with embarrassment. Thankfully, Ryan didn't seem to be offended by her brazen nature.

"Sorry," she said.

"For what?"

"I just…" she murmured. "I couldn't help myself."

"Aren't you supposed to be engaged?" he asked.

"Yes," Serena said, frowning. "I am. Don't you think it odd that I'd feel the urge to kiss you?"

"I can't say. Do you usually kiss men you barely know?"

Serena nodded. "All the time. I mean, I do on-screen. That's part of the job. But you're not…" She sank back into the seat. She had her answer. She hadn't just enjoyed the kiss, she was desperate to kiss him again. And she didn't want to stop there. She imagined tearing off his shirt and touching his body, kissing him in places that only she could discover.

She reached for the whiskey and took a big gulp, wincing as the liquor burned a path down her throat.

"I always wondered how that worked," Ryan said. "How do you kiss someone when it's just for show?"

"Are you asking if I get turned on?"

He shrugged. "I would think that would be one of the dangers."

"That's why so many actors end up together after they've worked on a film. At some point, the kissing starts to feel real."

"Is that what happened with you and…"

"Ben," she said. "Ben Thayer."

"Right. Ben."

"I suppose that's how it started. He was a really good kisser. And I got a bit swept away." But she'd never felt quite so infatuated as she was feeling now, sitting next to Ryan Quinn and imagining the next kiss they might share.

"I don't expect he'd be happy that you kissed me."

"Hmm." She smiled at him. "I suppose not. If you don't tell, I won't, either. We'll just make it our little secret." She needed time and space to be able to figure out what all this meant, and right now she had neither.

"Secrets can be very dangerous," Ryan said.

Serena took another sip of the whiskey, then handed him the glass. "Tell me one of your secrets," she said. "As an actor, I've become quite keen at observation. And I believe you're the kind of man who keeps his secrets buried very deep."

"What you see is what you get," Ryan said with a shrug. He gave her a sideways glance, then shook his head. "I'm not here for your amusement."

"Of course not," she replied.

"And I won't make you do anything you don't want to do."

"Thank you." She picked up the glass, then got to her feet. "I think we're going to have a lot of fun this week. If I were you, Quinn, I'd get some sleep. I intend to keep you very busy."

Serena wandered back to her seat. Miles gave her a suspicious look as she passed him, and she rolled her eyes. "I was just being friendly."

But when she'd settled into her own spot, she closed her eyes and sighed. She couldn't seem to put the memories of her kiss with Ryan Quinn out of her mind. Even now, her heart was still beating a bit faster than normal, and her breathing had grown shallow and short.

Her gaze dropped to the six-carat diamond ring that sparkled on her finger. She was due to walk down the aisle in just a few weeks. Everything was planned. Two hundred and fifty guests had all received their invitations. And yet she wasn't thinking about the man waiting for her at home in Los Angeles. Instead, she was obsessing over the man sitting just a few feet away.

It was proof that she didn't love Ben. But then, she'd never really believed in true love, anyway, so what had changed? When it came down to it, was one kiss reason enough to destroy her chance at happiness? "Get a grip," she muttered to herself. Ryan was a distraction. Ben was the man she intended to marry.

A BRIGHTLY PAINTED VAN and a Peugeot sedan were waiting for them when the Learjet landed in Nadi, on the island of Viti Levu. They taxied to stop near a well-lit hangar, and Miles and Ryan helped the ladies gather their luggage and fill out their customs and immigration forms for the waiting official. When they were cleared, the girls stumbled into the van, still half-asleep.

"Please tell me we're finally here," one of the women cried.

"You're here," Ryan said.

He glanced at Serena, and she smiled warmly before disappearing into the van.

Miles and Ryan decided to ride in the sedan, chauffeured by a smiling Fijian. He held out his hand as they approached. "I am Arthur Cawaru. I manage the house at Bellavista."

Ryan shook his hand. "I'm Ryan Quinn. Thom said you'd be able to help me out with the arrangements."

"I am at your service, Mr. Quinn."

Miles introduced himself to Arthur and they got into the rear seat of the car. Though the sun wasn't up yet, the eastern sky had begun to change from black to a deep blue, and the stars had started to fade. They drove on narrow, winding roads that hugged the coast, the South Pacific on one side and lush, tropical vegetation on the other.

Ryan chuckled softly. "This is bloody brilliant."

"Brilliant?"

"Look at us. Someone is paying us to hang out in this tropical paradise with five beautiful women. It's like we won the lottery."

"I wouldn't jump the gun on that," Miles said.

Ryan glanced over at him. "What do you mean?"

"You don't know Serena. She can be…a handful. She's gorgeous and talented. But she's also mercurial and stubborn. And moody and demanding. One moment she seems smarter than any woman you've ever met, and then she'll do something that defies common sense, and you wonder how she can be so clueless. If she weren't so damn beautiful and good at what she does, she wouldn't get work."

"She can't be that bad," Ryan said.

"She's got lots of baggage," Miles murmured. "Just don't get caught up in the fantasy. She's nothing like she is on the screen."

"I've never seen her movies."

Miles stared at him in disbelief. "Never?"

"Was that part of the job?"

"No. Maybe it's for the best. You won't be captivated by her."

Ryan chuckled softly. It was too late for that, he mused. "Hey, I'm always a professional, and I made a promise to Mr. Perry. No worries there."

"She's a professional, too," Miles said. "She's an actress and a good one. So take everything she says with a grain of salt."

The rest of the ride passed in silence. Ryan found it difficult to reconcile the woman Miles was talking about with the woman he'd met on the plane. He'd found Serena sweet and charming and vulnerable. And yet to hear Miles tell it, Serena Hightower was trouble. For Miles, anything that interfered with the box office profits of Thom Perry's latest movie would be cause for concern. To both Miles and Thom, Serena was a commodity, an investment that would pay off only if she behaved to their standards.

The sedan turned off the main road, and after a few minutes, they drove through a tall gate. A moment later, a sprawling mansion appeared out of the dark, the white exterior lit by floodlights. "Crikey," Ryan murmured. "This is a bit more posh than the tents I usually sleep in."

"We thought it might be better if Ms. Hightower and her party stayed at a private villa instead of a resort," Miles explained. "That way we can control the environment."

"What do you expect they'll be doing? Pillaging the villages? Stealing cars and raping the menfolk?"

"It's always best to expect the worst," Miles said.

The vehicles pulled around the large circular drive and stopped at the grand entrance to the house. Ryan hopped out and Miles followed him. A Fijian woman appeared at the door with a tray of drinks, each decorated with a fresh flower.

"Welcome to Bellavista," Arthur said in his booming voice. "This is my wife, Juni. House cook. She will bring you anything you would like to eat."

Juni handed them each a glass. "Wonderful," Miles muttered. "More alcohol."

"Fruit juice," Juni whispered, "with ginseng. Good for jet lag."

The girls walked into the house, one by one, sipping at their drinks. When they were all inside, Ryan followed. He introduced himself to Juni, then trailed after Miles, slowly turning as he took in the luxurious interior. "Nice crib," he murmured to himself.

"Thom bought it five years ago," Miles commented.

"Thom owns this?"

"Yeah. He's got a château in France, a condo in New York, a beach house in L.A., a mansion in Beverly Hills and a place in Aspen. And this. Strange thing is, he hardly has time to vacation. I don't think he's been here in two or three years. But it's a handy place to stash the occasional detoxing actor or actress. Very private. Virtually no media presence on the island."

"Mr. Quinn, your room is this way," Arthur said. "Mr. DuMont, please follow Juni. You're in the other wing."

Arthur reached for Ryan's bag, but he shook his head. "I've got it."

"This way."

His room was airy and spacious, the windows covered with large floor-to-ceiling shutters. Ryan tossed his gear on the bed, then threw open the shutters and walked out onto a wide terrace that overlooked the ocean. It was still dark, but the sound of the surf filled the air.

"I love the way it smells here. What is that? I can't place the scent."

Ryan turned to the right and found Serena sitting on the stone wall nearby, staring out at the eastern horizon. She had the room right next to his.

"Frangipani, I think," Ryan replied. "They're most fragrant at night. They don't have nectar, but they use their scent to trick moths into pollinating them. The poor moth does all the work for no reward."

"Well, I'm impressed."

"My mother has been trying to grow frangipani for years without any success." He decided a change of subject was in order. "I figured you'd crawl right into bed. It's been a long trip."

She smiled. "No. I can sleep later. I wanted to watch the sunrise." She pointed out at the water. "Look. It's about to happen."

A tiny sliver of red light appeared over the water and they both stared at it. Though they were standing a fair distance away from each other, Ryan felt oddly close to her, as if they'd discovered a connection between them.

As the sun crept higher, it painted the clouds in a blaze of purple and orange. Ryan had seen a lot of sunrises in a lot of beautiful places, but this one was different. He felt as if he couldn't breathe, as if his senses had suddenly cleared and his mind had sharpened. He should have been exhausted, but instead, he was energized.

"Do you ever wonder if you're living someone else's life?" she asked.

Ryan frowned, then turned and braced his hip against the wall. "Yeah. Sometimes."

It was as if she could read his mind. He'd been feeling like that a lot lately—as if he was living his father's life, or maybe his brothers'. He was tired of doing things just to please them. But while he'd like to hope he might open that surf school one day, Ryan could barely support himself on what he made. And despite his refusal to join them on the Everest expedition, he couldn't abandon his brothers when they needed him.

"I don't know how—or when—I lost control of my own life," Serena continued. "I'm not sure I ever even had it. God, I'm tired of pretending."

He heard the exhaustion in her voice and he wanted to go to her and comfort her in some way. But he knew better than to touch her again. "Isn't that what an actor does for a living?" Ryan asked.

"When the camera is on. But I pretend to be someone I'm not even when the camera is off." She swung her legs around and jumped off the wall onto the terrace. "This isn't what you signed on for, is it? Listening to me moan about how horrible my life is."

"Usually I'm worried about my clients tumbling down the side of a mountain or falling into a crevasse. I think I can manage listening to your problems."

Serena nodded. "Yes, you're the kind of man who can handle just about anything, aren't you? You seem very...

competent." She walked over to him, then looked up to meet his gaze. "I'm sorry about the kiss. I was just—I don't know. I shouldn't have done that."

Ryan knew he should be sorry, too. He hated people who didn't take their promises seriously. But as his gaze drifted down to her lips he found that he wanted to kiss her again, to drag her into his arms and see where it all might lead. It didn't even matter that she was supposed to walk down the aisle in less than a month.

Besides being engaged, she was also completely out of his league, Ryan mused. Guys like him didn't date movie stars. "Hey, I can go home and tell everyone I kissed Serena Hightower. Not that I'll tell anyone. I won't. But, occasionally, I might think about it. The kiss, not telling people about it."

"I suppose that wouldn't be so bad," she said. "I might do the same." She drew a ragged breath and closed her eyes. "I need some sleep. I'll talk to you later." She took a step closer and brushed a kiss on his cheek. "Thank you, Quinn."

"For what?"

"For…listening," she said. "No one ever does."

She walked back inside and Ryan watched her leave, admiring the gentle sway of her hips as she moved. He was left wondering about the things she'd confessed to him. Was she really that unhappy with her life? She was supposedly in love. She had a great career and plenty of money. Everyone knew her name and her face. She flew around the world on private jets and stayed in mansions on tropical islands.

"Yeah, she's out of your league," he muttered. "Off limits."

Ryan groaned softly, then rubbed his hands over his tired eyes. This was unlike any other trip he'd worked. But the goals were the same. Keep the client happy. So if Serena wanted to talk, then he was there to listen. If she wanted to hike, he was there to guide her. And if she wanted to kiss him again...he'd have to draw the line there.

Kissing a client would be considered a breach in the company rules against fraternization—and his own. But thinking about kissing her wasn't. He could go a long time rewinding what had happened on the plane and imagining what could have happened if they'd both been free to do more.

2

SERENA ROLLED OVER in bed and squinted at the clock. From the light filtering through the shutters, she could tell that it was closer to noon than to midnight. She'd slept for five hours without moving and she felt perfectly refreshed.

They'd spend a week on Fiji, and though this was technically her hen party, in truth, she didn't feel much like celebrating. Instead, she wanted to distract herself with exercise and adventure. Perhaps that was the best way to calm what Thom called her "prewedding jitters."

"Jitters," she murmured. Serena held out her hand. She wasn't jittery. She felt a sense of calm now that she'd put an entire ocean between herself and the wedding plans. She could almost pretend it wasn't happening.

She smiled, remembering her conversation with Ryan Quinn. The idea of spending the next week with him was more appealing than spending it with her four bridesmaids. And just because she enjoyed his company, didn't mean she was cheating.

Unfortunately, Ben didn't have the same loyalty to her. He'd strayed twice in the past year, both times with married costars. The tabloids had printed the rumors but hadn't been able to confirm them, and Serena had almost convinced herself that his behavior was indeed part of his "process." In order to play a believable romantic scene on-screen, Ben claimed he needed to experience real romance with his costar.

She frowned. Why did that suddenly seem so disingenuous? Was it because her doubts about their pending marriage were growing deeper with every day that passed? Was it because she was searching for a way out and the clock was ticking down?

Cursing softly, Serena rolled out of bed and rummaged through her suitcase for a pair of shorts and a T-shirt. She slipped into a pair of sport sandals, then grabbed a band and gathered her tousled hair into a ponytail. Her sunglasses were tucked in her purse, and she pulled them out and put them on top of head.

The housekeeper, Juni, was in the kitchen and offered Serena some lunch when she walked through. Serena politely declined, instead grabbing a banana and a bottle of water. "Have you seen Ryan?"

"He said he was going to take a walk on the beach," Juni said. "The other ladies are at the pool, enjoying mimosas. And Mr. Miles is in the office on the phone."

She wandered out onto the rear terrace and headed to the pool. Her bridesmaids were dressed in colorful bikinis and sprawled on cushioned chaises. "Let the adventure begin," Serena called.

They all groaned. "Have a drink," Arabella insisted,

her glass dangling from her fingers. "It'll help with the hangover and the jet lag. And your infernal enthusiasm."

Serena settled onto a chair and turned her face up to the sun, but before long, she sighed impatiently. "We can't spend the entire week lying about like this. It's a crashing bore."

Caroline sat up and glanced around. "We could go shopping. I'm up for that."

"We can shop at home. Don't you want to explore the island? We're in Fiji. There are jungles and volcanoes and—well, I don't know what else. I want to see something amazing."

"Do they have a Tiffany's here? We could go look at diamonds," Cecily said. "They're amazing."

"Have a drink, Serena," Lizzy said. "Relax"

A long silence descended over the group. Maybe they were right. Maybe she should just relax for a day and let everyone decompress from the flight. Then they'd all want to do something tomorrow.

"Who is that?" Lizzy asked, tugging her sunglasses down and staring toward the beach. "Is that our pool boy? Oh, my, I call dibs. That man is going to be in my bed tonight."

"Then I get him tomorrow night," Arabella said.

Serena sat up and gazed toward the beach, then smiled. "That's not the pool boy, that's Quinn." All four girls turned and looked at her for further explanation. "Ryan Quinn? He was on the plane with us last night. He helped you with your bags?"

"He's the butler?" Lizzy asked.

"He's the adventure guide," Serena said. She waved

to him as he approached, taking a moment to admire the sight. He was dressed in board shorts and nothing more. His tanned chest was muscled, his shoulders wide. He looked impossibly fit but not the fit that came from hours with a trainer. His skin gleamed with a sheen of sweat, and it looked as if he'd been running on the beach.

"Bloody hell, Serena, you're drooling."

Serena glanced over at Caroline. "What?"

"Hi," Ryan said as he climbed the steps to the pool terrace. His gaze was fixed on her and he didn't seem to notice the other four women there.

"Good morning," she said. "Or afternoon."

"Did you sleep well?" he asked, a smile twitching at the corners of his mouth. Her heart skipped and Serena drew a deep breath. He was so much sexier in the light of day.

"I did. Sleep. But now I'm ready for some excitement. Adventure." She cleared her throat. "Ryan, let me introduce you to my bridesmaids. Lizzy Stanton is on the end. And that's Arabella Moulton-Gray," she continued. "This is my maid of honor, Cecily Winston. And that's Caroline Pentwell."

"Hello," Ryan said, gifting them all with a charming smile. "It's nice to meet you. I've got a great plan for this afternoon if you're up for it."

Serena nodded. "Absolutely."

"When would you like to go?" he asked.

"Now," Serena said. "I'm ready now."

"Let me change and I'll meet you all out front in ten

minutes. Wear sturdy shoes." He glanced down at Serena's feet. "Like those."

He waved and walked to the house, five pairs of eyes fixed on his retreat.

"That man needs an agent. He is all kinds of hot," Arabella said. She turned to Serena. "And you, my darling Serena, are smitten."

Serena gasped. "What?"

"Totally smitten," Cecily said. "So, how was he in bed?"

"I did not sleep with him!" Serena cried.

"Then what was all that talk about sleeping well?" Caroline asked. "And that stare. He looked like he was about to devour you."

"In case you've all forgotten, I'm getting married next month."

"Yeah, but you don't love Ben," Arabella said.

Serena frowned. "What—what makes you say that?"

"You never talk about him," Cecily said. "You haven't mentioned him once since we left L.A. We understand. It's all for show. And it's a great PR move. We'll play our part."

"I'd do the same if I had the chance," Caroline said. "And after a while, you just get a divorce. It's no big deal. Every great actress goes through a few marriages before she finds the one that works."

"Besides, *Ben* messes around," Cecily said. "You should be able to have some fun of your own."

Serena scrambled off her chaise. "It's not like that. And I am not smitten with Ryan Quinn. Now get up and get dressed. We're going on an adventure." She spun around and stalked toward the house. They were right. She didn't love Ben. She'd been able to convince herself she did, at first, but somewhere between the cheating and the time apart, she'd realized what she really wanted.

She'd fallen for the fantasy, the security of love and marriage, the happily-ever-after. Her parents, both actors, had divorced when she was six and had stumbled through a long series of affairs and marriages. Why had she thought she'd be any different?

She stopped and turned around, then strode back to the girls when she realized they weren't following. "Are you coming or not?"

Lizzy waved her off. "Let's just say we did and stay here. I'm still working on my hangover from last night and the jet lag is starting to set in."

"Count me out," Caroline said.

"Me, too," Lizzy added.

Serena frowned. "Bella, you'll come, right?"

Arabella groaned. "Maybe tomorrow, Serena. I really want to work on my tan. A real tan is so much nicer than a spray tan, and I'm just so white right now. But you go, if you want. Sounds like...fun." She lowered her sunglasses. "Just be careful. You don't want a guy like that going to the tabloids and telling all."

"I'm not going to sleep with him," Serena shouted. "God, you are the worst bridesmaids in the world." When she got into the house, Juni was waiting for her with a large basket. "A picnic," she said. "In case you get hungry?"

Serena took the basket from her. "Thank you. That was thoughtful."

"He is waiting out front. Are the others coming?"

"No, they just want to rest."

Juni frowned, her eyebrow arching. "Not very good bridesmaids, I'd say."

Serena laughed. "No, Juni, not good at all."

She passed Miles in the hall. "I'm leaving."

"Wait. Let me grab the camera and I'll come along," he said.

"No need. My bridesmaids are staying behind. It's just me and Ryan."

"Alone? Just the two of you?" Miles asked. "Wait a moment. Are you really sure you should—"

"Don't worry, Miles. I'll behave myself."

She found Ryan leaning casually against the van parked in the circular drive. She handed him the basket, then pointed to the Jeep parked behind it. "Do you have the keys?" she asked.

"I think they're already inside," he replied. "But we can't take that. There's not enough room."

"It's just going to be you and me," she said. "And I'll drive. But we've got to move quick or we'll have to take Miles." She hopped in behind the wheel and waited for him to get inside.

He tossed his day pack in the backseat, then tucked the basket in a spot on the floor before sliding into the passenger seat.

"Forget my lazy bridesmaids." She reached for the ignition, and the Jeep roared to life. Serena smiled. "Who cares about them? I'm going to do what I want to do."

With a hoot, she threw the Jeep into gear and pressed the accelerator to the floor just as Miles emerged from the front door.

Right now, she wanted to forget about the wedding and Ben and the mess that she'd created. She wanted to forget about her bridesmaids and publicity photos and her career. Serena wanted a lovely day with sunshine and happiness and beauty. She'd decide about the rest of it later.

IT WAS THE perfect day, Ryan mused. The sky was blue, the air was warm and the scents of Fiji filled his head. And for once, he planned to have some fun on the job.

He was usually worried about one thing or another in his professional life, but what could go wrong today? No one was going to fall off a mountainside, no one was going to freeze to death or succumb to altitude sickness. And he had an entire afternoon with Serena Hightower.

Ryan knew he had to ignore his attraction, or at least control it. So he'd decided to admire her from a distance and keep his feelings to himself. He'd be a professional and wouldn't let his attraction show.

He didn't have to remind himself that she was engaged. That fact was firmly embedded in his brain. And yet the moment he looked at her, Ryan forgot all about that wall between them. Instead, his mind was hijacked with thoughts of seduction, of casting aside moral objections and letting passion take over.

He drew a deep breath and made a silent vow to behave himself.

She drove along the coastal highway for a few kilometers, then turned inland, smoothly navigating the curves as they headed into the hills. Ryan gave her directions, and they left the paved road and started down a narrow dirt track cut out of the thick rain forest.

"Sorry about the other girls," Serena said. "They're really not the hiking sort."

"This is your hen party. Shouldn't they do what you want to do? I thought that was their duty as bridesmaids and as friends."

"They're not really my friends. I mean, I know them, but we're not friends."

"I don't understand."

"My wedding planner picked them. Mostly because they looked great in the dresses she chose. They agreed because it's great publicity for them. And I really didn't care."

Was she just exaggerating or was this the truth? Did she have no friends of her own? She was sweet and funny and seemed as though she'd attract friends as easily as she'd attracted him. But then, Ryan could answer only for the males in the crowd.

He glanced over and stole a long look. She was dressed in a simple T-shirt and hiking shorts, her hair in a ponytail, pulled away from her pretty face. He studied her profile—the perfectly set eyes, the straight nose, the lush lips. She was Hollywood beauty. But yet, in this setting, without makeup and a fancy dress, she seemed normal…approachable.

He found the contrast intriguing. Who was this woman who could so easily exist in both his world and that strange, glamorous world of the movies? The more he got to know her, the more complicated she became.

They found the trail to the waterfall he'd researched earlier, and Serena pulled the car into a small clearing and switched off the ignition. Ryan grabbed his day pack and slung it over his shoulder, then picked up the picnic basket.

Since the waterfall was a local secret, the path wasn't well-worn, and Ryan had to watch carefully so that they didn't wander in the wrong direction. "What about your real friends?" he asked, reaching out to help her over a muddy spot. "You must have had someone *you* wanted to pick as a bridesmaid. A sister?"

"I'm an only child." She glanced over at him. "And I don't really have a lot of friends," Serena explained. "I've always been a bit of a loner." She shrugged indifferently. He could see that talking about the past troubled her. "I know. It sounds pathetic, but I grew up with parents who were always on one movie set or another. When I was with either my mom or dad on set, I had a tutor, and I hung around adults all day long. When I was at home, I played with the housekeeper. I just never figured out how to make friends. Or maybe I never wanted friends."

"Who do you hang out with now? When you're not working on a movie?"

"There's Ben. But mostly my dogs."

"And they don't look good in the dresses?" Ryan teased.

"I have five dogs," she said, giggling. "And I would have had them as attendants, but the wedding planner wouldn't allow it. They're all rescues. They live at my country house outside London. My housekeeper takes care of them when I'm gone. Do you have dogs?"

"One. Duffy. He lives with my sister, Dana, most of the time, but he stays with me or my brothers when we're home."

"You should get more dogs. One is not enough. Lots of dogs need adopting."

He held out his hand to her again, to help her over a steep spot on the path. But this time, he didn't let go. The track widened and they were able to walk side by side up a gentle rise, their pace slowing. In the distance, Ryan heard the sound of water.

"I think we're getting close." Serena pulled him along the path, and a few moments later, they emerged into a clearing. A soft gasp slipped from her lips and she sighed. They stood at the edge of a clear pool. Above him, water cascaded off a rock cliff and tumbled into the far edge of the pool. "It's beautiful."

Ryan had become a bit jaded when it came to natural beauty. He'd seen some of the most extraordinary sights in the world, and he'd always felt the need to rank them in order of perfection, rather than simply enjoy the sight. This was different. He could relax and enjoy what he was seeing. "It is bloody awesome."

"Good job," she said, bumping his shoulder with hers. She started toward the edge of the pond. "Do you think if we climb up there, we could jump into the water?"

"There's supposed to be a spot for that on the right," he explained, dropping his day pack. "But maybe we ought to leave the jumping for another day. If you crack your head, I'd have to carry you out of here and—"

"You promised me adventure. I want adventure."

"All right, but first we should make sure the pool is deep enough."

She tugged her T-shirt over her head, and to Ryan's surprise, she wasn't wearing a bikini—she was wearing a lacy black bra. Her shorts came off next, revealing a leopard-print thong. To his great relief, she didn't remove anything else, and he drew a shaky breath as she walked toward the edge of the pool.

Serena turned around and motioned to him. "Come on."

He had made a promise to himself, and Ryan Quinn always kept his promises. He yanked off his T-shirt and followed her. She grabbed his hand and pulled him into the water with her, gliding out into the center of the pool, their fingers still linked.

"Let me check the depth. I'll be right back," he said. Ryan dove beneath the surface, moving down, away from the light. The water was clear, though, and he could easily gauge the distance to the bottom of the pool. He came to the surface, beneath the rock ledge. "It looks good."

She swam over to him. "I'm glad I have you to look after me."

"Just doing my job, miss."

"And you do it so well."

Serena crawled out of the pool and began to scale the rocks to the right of the waterfall. Ryan climbed up behind her, watching to make sure her footing was secure along the way. She moved with an easy grace and a confidence that surprised him. That was becoming a pattern with Serena. She was always surprising him.

When they reached the ledge, Serena held out her hand. "We have to jump together," she said.

"All right," Ryan said. "You count it down."

She drew a deep breath. "Three. Two. One."

They leaped off the twenty-foot ledge and fell into the pool, the water rushing up and over them as they broke the surface. Ryan lost his hold on Serena's hand but felt her body brush against his as he kicked toward the light. She was laughing when he came up in front of her.

Ryan stared into her pretty face, noticing the droplets of water clinging to her lashes. He reached out and smoothed a strand of hair off her cheek, and she turned into his touch, her eyelids fluttering.

Every instinct urged him to kiss her, to take advantage of the moment and forget all that was keeping them apart. But she was engaged, and until she told him differently, he intended to respect that.

"I can't believe you made that jump," he said, swimming away from her. "I guess you were right to ask for an adventure guide."

"Uh-oh." She reached beneath the surface and, a moment later, raised her hand, her torn bra dangling from her fingertips. "This didn't survive the fall," she said, tossing it onto the shore.

Ryan groaned inwardly. Was she tempting him on purpose? "You shouldn't have done that," he warned.

Serena looked at him, a quizzical arch to her eyebrow. "Everyone on the planet has seen me naked, Quinn. I'm sure you looked me up on Google and found the pictures."

"What pictures?"

"*The* pictures. Of me and one of my former boyfriends, having a bit of a romp on a yacht in the Mediterranean." She frowned. "You haven't seen them?"

"Nope."

Her gaze narrowed and she observed him suspiciously. "How much do you know about me?"

"I know that you're an actress and you have a movie coming out after Christmas and you're getting married before the movie comes out."

"Have you ever watched one of my films?" she asked.

Ryan winced, then shook his head. "I plan on watching them all when I get home. But right now…no, not a one."

"You're lying."

"I don't go to the movies much. At least not in the last seven or eight years. I spend most of my time in places that don't have television or movie theatres—or running water."

"Turn around," she said, pointing at him. "Right now. Turn around."

Ryan did as he was told. He heard splashing behind him and he smiled. He didn't have to see her; he could imagine exactly what she looked like, emerging from the pool, almost naked, her wet body gleaming in the shafts of sunlight that broke through the cover of the trees.

Though he had vowed to fight the temptations of her body, Ryan risked a glance, then immediately regretted it. She stood on the shore, her back to him. His gaze skimmed her body from her shoulders to the sweet curves of her backside, then along her shapely legs. She was like some water nymph, a creature from a magical world.

He felt his body react, so Ryan spun away and swam toward the waterfall. He dove beneath the surface and stroked hard until he reached the edge of the pool, trying to forget the image burned in his brain.

"All right," she called. "I'm decent."

Ryan turned around and swam back to the other side of the pool. "Thank you."

"Sorry," she said. "I usually don't have any inhibitions when it comes to nudity. When you've gone starkers on the big screen, there's not much mystery left."

"I can just imagine," he murmured.

THEY SPENT THE entire afternoon at the waterfall. Ryan retrieved the picnic basket from the Jeep and they opened a bottle of wine and sat on a blanket at the edge of the pool, watching the sunlight sparkle across the surface of the water.

"It's been a perfect day, Quinn," Serena murmured, drawing her knees up to her chest and fixing her gaze on her handsome companion. "I can't remember the last time I had so much fun, doing something I wanted to do." She paused, then reached out and placed her hand on his arm. "Thank you."

"I try to please," Ryan said.

"I wish we could stay here. You could build us a nice little hut right over there. I could raise some chickens. We could have a simple life."

"You don't have to stay here to have a simple life," he suggested.

There were times when Serena thought that Ryan understood her perfectly. And then, there were moments like this one, when she realized they lived in completely different worlds.

Ben, on the other hand, understood the life of a professional actor, the choices she'd had to make, the difficulties of being a celebrity. That's one of the reasons why she'd agreed to marry him.

"Tell me about this man of yours," Ryan said, stretching out on the blanket. He lay on his side and watched her silently, as if he were able to read her mind.

"I don't want to talk about Ben," Serena said, shaking her head.

"You're marrying him in a few weeks. I'd think you'd want to talk about him. Or the wedding. Or your plans for the future."

She didn't want to argue with him if he was determined to force the issue. "All right, what do you want to know? Ask me anything. I can tell you about the flower arrangements and the groomsmen's gifts. I can describe my dress and—"

"Why are you not wearing your ring?" Ryan said, pointing to her hand.

"I—I left it in my room," she said. "I didn't want to lose it."

"Is that the real reason?"

What did he want her to say? Did he want her to admit that she was attracted to him? "No," she finally said. "I guess I just wanted to forget the wedding for an afternoon."

"Are you having doubts?"

She laughed softly, then covered her face with her hands. "It's too late to have doubts, Quinn. I can't back out now. Everything is planned. And I already have a reputation as a reckless nitwit—a reputation that was well earned when I was younger. But that's not me now. People are just starting to take me seriously."

"Is that why you said yes?"

"I also really wanted to believe I was in love and that I could finally have something…normal. That I wouldn't be alone anymore."

"So call it off," Ryan said.

She couldn't look at him. If she did, she wouldn't be able to resist him any longer. She was fighting so hard against this attraction. It should be easy, but there was something so comforting about him. Though she barely knew him, Serena sensed that she could trust him.

"My life would be a shambles if I did." She sat up, drawing a deep breath and gathering her resolve. "I'm going to get married. And in a year or two, if it becomes impossible to carry on, I'll get a divorce. No one will be surprised. Hollywood marriages never work out the first time."

"And that's what you think you deserve?" Ryan asked.

"No. But it's my fault I let it get this far. It's a runaway train now. I can't stop it without the entire thing going off the rails. So many people will be upset with me."

"But it's your life," Ryan said. "You do what makes you happy."

"How many people are really happy with their lives? We all make sacrifices and compromises," Serena said. "Are you completely happy with your life, Quinn?"

Ryan considered her question for a long moment. "Not entirely," he said. "But I'm planning to make some changes." He cursed softly, shaking his head. "So, where should we put this hut? Over there? Or there?"

Serena lay down, stretching out opposite him and meeting his gaze. "Why aren't you happy?"

"There have been lots of changes lately."

"Like?"

"Both of my brothers are settling down and getting married. I'm not real happy with my job. I need a change, but I can't afford to do what I want to do. And then, my brothers are trying to talk me into climbing Everest, and I'm not real keen on the idea."

"Isn't that what you do?"

"My father was a climber and he died on Everest. They found his body last spring and we're supposed to go up there to retrieve his personal effects. But it's opening a lot of old wounds that never completely healed."

"Wow," she murmured. "And I thought my wedding problems were bad."

She placed her hand between her and Ryan, her fingers splayed across the blanket, just inches from his face. Serena wanted to touch him, to run her hand over his face. Her fingers trembled and a moment later, Ryan covered her hand with his.

It was such a simple point of contact, and yet it

seemed even more intimate than a kiss or a caress. How much longer could she fight this attraction to him? It was wrong, yet it felt right. But was it real? Was she just transferring her hopes for normalcy and belonging from Ben to Ryan? Or was there something between them that went beyond a sexual attraction? That was the question Serena couldn't answer.

"It's feels so odd when you touch me," she murmured, her gaze fixed on his hand. He drew his hand away, but she caught his fingers and laced them through hers. "Am I cheating?"

"I don't know," Ryan said. "Are you?"

"I feel like I am."

"Then we should stop," Ryan said.

She yanked her hand away and sat up. "You're right. We should probably go. It's getting late and the girls are going to wonder where we are. Miles is probably ready to call the local police."

"Would it make it easier if I left Fiji?" Ryan asked. "I can. I'll call one of my brothers, and he could be on a plane in a few hours, to take over. I can assure you, they're not nearly as charming as I am."

Serena knew she ought to accept his offer. It was the only safe thing to do. But in her heart, she didn't think it would make a difference. She'd already started down this road—the road away from Ben and toward Ryan—and with every step, she was more determined not to turn back.

"No," she said. "We can control our impulses. But maybe we should make sure that we don't spend a lot of time alone."

"You're right," he said. "If the girls don't want to come along, we'll bring Miles."

"It's a plan," she said.

"There is one thing I'd like to say before we leave."

"Do I want to hear it?" Serena asked.

"Probably not. But I'm going to say it anyway. You deserve to be happy. You deserve everything good in life, and you shouldn't settle for anything less."

"So you think I should call off the wedding, Quinn?"

"I can't tell you to do that," Ryan said.

"Of course you can," Serena countered. "Just say it. Say 'Serena, call off the wedding.' It's not that hard. Everyone has an opinion."

"Everyone does."

"Say it," Serena insisted.

"I can't. I won't."

"Why not?"

"Because I have less noble reasons for saying something like that. Because I want to kiss you again. I want to touch you without feeling guilty. And I don't want to be the bloke who ruined your wedding."

Serena stood up. "See? This is my problem. No one ever tells me the truth. They only tell me what they think I want to hear. I can't make my own decisions. I never have been able to. I'm the princess of self-doubt. And now, when I am finally ready to make a decision, everyone is telling me not to. So just give me the truth. Tell me that I can call off this wedding and it might be messy for a while but everything will be all right."

She saw the conflict in his expression, and Serena understood his reluctance to get involved. He was right.

What man wanted to be responsible for breaking up the current Hollywood supercouple? No doubt word would leak out about the cause of her abandoned wedding. There were four women on this trip who would gladly sell the story to the tabloids. And he had his own reputation to worry about.

"All right," she said. "I understand. I'm being ridiculous."

"Serena, I—"

"No," she said, pressing a finger to his lips. "This has been a pleasant little diversion, but you're right. We'll keep our distance and always have a chaperone."

"If that's what you want," he said. "At the end of the week, I'll just tell Thom that you wanted to relax and that the adventure part of the trip didn't happen."

Serena nodded. It was a reasonable compromise. And it gave her time. She had to make her own decisions. Right now, she had no idea what she was going to do, but by the end of the week, she'd have it all sorted out.

3

THE SUN WAS just barely over the horizon when Ryan walked into the kitchen. Juni and Arthur were enjoying their breakfast, but both of them got to their feet when he entered. "Sit," Ryan said. "I can get my own coffee." He poured himself a mug and joined them at the table.

"What can I make you for breakfast?" Juni asked.

He pointed to a plate of fresh bread. "I'll have a bit of that? What is it?"

"Bibingka," Juni said. "It is a bread made of cassava, coconut cream, eggs and cheese. I've made scones for the misses. And I have fresh papaya and mango. May I make you an omelet?"

"No, this sounds good, thanks," Ryan said. He grabbed a piece of the *bibingka* and took a bite. "Umm. I've never eaten anything quite like this. It's delicious."

Arthur nodded. "My wife makes excellent *bibingka.* A tasty prawn curry, too. She is a very good cook."

There was pride and affection in Arthur's smile. He'd seen that same look on Mal's face when he talked about

Amy, and in Rogan's expression when he spoke about Claudia. It was like some secret knowledge that men had when they were in love, and until now, he hadn't really understood. But now he did.

He felt the same when he thought about Serena, about all the qualities that made her such an amazing woman. And he wasn't even in love with her.

"Have another," Juni said, holding out the plate of *bibingka.* Startled out of his thoughts, Ryan accepted the offer. He made a mental note to ask Juni to recommend some Fijian restaurants. Now that he had more time, he could enjoy everything the island had to offer, including its cuisine. But first he had to work up an appetite.

"Arthur, I'd like to go surfing today. I understand there are some awesome reef breaks off Nadi, but I need to get a board."

"Mr. Thom has some surfboards," Arthur said. "I'm sure he wouldn't mind if you used them. I'll get them out for you."

"Could you? Thanks. I'd like to go this morning, if possible."

"There is a good place for beginners called Resorts Left near Nadi. And an easy beach break at Sigatoka."

"I'm looking for something intermediate or better. The girls aren't interested in doing anything today, so I figured I'd take advantage of the free time."

"No problems," the other man said with a wide smile. "I will make arrangements for you. You'll need a boat to get you to and from the reef. I have a friend."

"Thank you, Arthur. I'd appreciate that."

"There is also a great spot to windsurf at the mouth of the Sigatoka River; you must try that while you are here. Mr. Thom has a windsurfer, as well."

"Maybe I'll give that a go tomorrow."

"I will check into that boat."

"And I will make you a big breakfast," Juni said. "You will need it for the day you are going to have."

Ryan wanted to get out of the house before the women woke up, hoping to avoid any uncomfortable encounters with Serena. Though they'd figured out a solution to their problem, it wasn't that easy living in the same house.

Last night he'd listened for her voice in the hall, waited for her footsteps outside his door. He'd spent the entire night staring at the ceiling and wondering if she was fighting the impulse to sneak into his room and continue what they'd started, just as he was.

At least once an hour, he'd got out of bed and walked to the door, ready to visit her room and tell her what he'd wanted to say at the waterfall. She shouldn't get married. She should walk away and wait for something better—like him.

But he couldn't fool himself. He wasn't her "something better" and he never would be. She lived in a different world, a world that he'd never understand. Occasionally, his life intersected with celebrity, but he wouldn't want it to on a permanent basis.

He'd always assumed that when he found the right woman, the "one," that it would all be so simple. He'd never thought she'd be in love with another man and that his attraction and affection would be wrong.

Ryan's father had carried on an affair, and his children were still feeling the repercussions of that affair twenty years later. Was that all he could expect from a relationship with Serena—false promises and secret encounters? Was that fair to the two of them? Or fair to her fiancé?

He'd known some blokes who messed about with married women, and they didn't seem to have any qualms about it. But Ryan couldn't rationalize that level of betrayal. Though there had been many qualities he'd admired in his father, infidelity had not been one of them.

Ryan had always been fiercely loyal to those he loved—his family, his friends. He'd never extended that loyalty toward a woman he'd dated. None of the women he'd dated had deserved it. But Serena was different. He wasn't sure what it was about her, and he couldn't explain the attraction, but it was there and it felt real and important.

"Juni, how long have you and Arthur been married?"

She placed a plate in front of him, an omelet filled with fresh vegetables and cheese. "For twenty-seven years," she said.

"Did you ever have any doubts? Maybe wonder if he wasn't the right guy for you?"

"If I'd had doubts, I wouldn't have married him," Juni said. "Doubts are like the waves. They come back again and again, until they wear you down and you're drowning in them. This is bad for a marriage."

"I agree," he said.

"Why do you ask a question like this? Is it because you are in love with Miss Serena?"

Ryan gasped. "Why would you think that?"

"It is quite clear. I can see it on your face when you look at her. But this is a dangerous game you play. She will break your heart. She is promised to another man."

"What if she decides not to marry him?"

"And what if she does marry him?"

Arthur walked back into the kitchen, putting an end to their conversation. "It is all arranged. You will meet my friend at his shop in Nadi. Here is a map to help you find your way."

"Where are you going?"

Ryan looked up to see Serena standing in the doorway. Her hair was windblown, and the color was high on her cheeks. He hadn't expected her to be up and about so early. "Good morning," he said.

She tipped her head, then sent him a shy smile. "Good morning, Quinn."

"Can I get you coffee or tea, miss?" Juni asked.

"Tea, please," she said. "Earl Grey tea, if you have it." Serena took a spot on the opposite side of the table. "You've made plans for today, Quinn?"

"I was going to go surfing. Arthur says there are some good reef breaks off Nadi. I thought I'd check them out."

"I've always wanted to learn how to surf," Serena said.

"These breaks are not for you, miss," Arthur said. "Very dangerous and only for experts. Try the beach break at Sigatoka. My oldest son learned to surf there."

Ryan met her gaze. The temptation was too great to ignore, and this was the job he'd promised Perry he'd do. "Do you want to go?"

She tipped her chin up and nodded. "Yes, I would like to go, if you'd like to teach me."

"I could do that," Ryan said.

"Then, I'll see if any of the others want to come along, as well. If not, we can leave right away."

Ryan nodded. "Arthur, can you draw me another map? And cancel that boat."

Arthur nodded. "Let me get the surfboards out. There is a rack for the top of the van."

"We'll probably take the Jeep," Ryan said, well familiar with Serena's bridesmaids.

Ryan and Arthur spent the next half hour setting up the rack and waxing the boards. By the time Serena returned, they were nearly ready to leave. Ryan hadn't expected Serena would be able to convince anyone to accompany her, so he was surprised when Cecily appeared at her side.

"Just you two?" Ryan asked.

"Yes, just us," Serena said. She hopped in the backseat of the Jeep and left the front seat to Cecily.

Ryan got behind the wheel. "Have you ever surfed before, Cecily?"

"Once," she said. "I nearly drowned. It was a nightmare."

"Really. And you want to try again?"

"No," she said. "But Serena insisted that one of us come along, and I lost."

Ryan glanced in the rearview mirror and caught Serena's gaze. "Well, I won't let you drown. And you may have fun. I'm an excellent teacher."

"I think I'll stay on the beach and watch," Cecily said.

"Come on," Serena said. "You have to give it a try, Ceci. Miles is going to come by later to take photos. Who knows, you could end up in *Us Weekly*."

"I suppose I could try," she said. "But I'm not going to get my hair wet. I paid seven hundred dollars for these highlights, and I don't want the seawater to ruin them."

Ryan smiled and winked at Serena. "That's the spirit," he said. "You'll love it, I promise."

A few minutes later, they were speeding along the coastal highway, headed into Nadi. Ryan wondered what was going through Serena's mind. Was she really interested in surfing, or did she want to spend the day with him and this was her way of keeping her end of the deal? He glanced back at her again and watched as she smoothed a strand of hair behind her ear. She was wearing her engagement ring again, the diamond flashing in the early morning light.

"Where are you from?" Cecily asked.

"New Zealand," Ryan replied.

"I have no idea where that is. Are you married?"

"No," Ryan said.

"Engaged? Involved?"

Ryan shook his head. "How about you?"

"I've given up on men. They're all worthless snakes and money-hungry leeches."

"Are we? I wasn't aware of that."

"I'm sure you think you're a lovely man, but it's in your genetics. You can't help yourself. You are programmed to break women's hearts."

"Cecily just broke up with her boyfriend," Serena explained. "He dumped her on Twitter. It was a big thing."

"They talked about it on *E! News,*" Cecily said. "It was so humiliating."

"What is *E! News?*" Ryan asked.

Cecily shook her head. "Where do you live? The moon?"

Ryan laughed. "No. New Zealand. I guess I need to start paying closer attention to these things. I didn't realize I was missing all this important news."

Cecily put on a pout, then turned to stare out the window. "If I drown, my agent will kill you both."

THEY FOUND THE beach with the help of Arthur's map. Cecily plopped down in the sand as Ryan and Serena ferried their equipment from the car park out to the water's edge.

Though Serena had watched a few surfing competitions when she spent a summer in Malibu, she didn't know much about the sport. She only half listened as Ryan explained the difference between the two types of surfboards he'd brought, choosing instead to focus on the way the morning sun gleamed on his sun-burnished chest.

The longboard was more stable and easier for a beginner to ride, while the shortboard was maneuverable but more difficult to balance on the wave, he explained, pointing out the fins on the bottom of each. "You'll learn on the longboard."

"And then I can try the short one?" she asked.

"No, I brought that one along for me. Arthur said there are some decent breaks just down the beach."

"So you're going to leave me here to flounder and drown."

"No," Ryan said. "You're going to exhaust yourself pretty quickly just trying to get up and stay up. You'll spend a lot more time in the water than on the board."

"You don't have much confidence in me, do you?" she muttered.

"I'm a good teacher, and I'll get you up. But surfing is a lot of work."

"Just watch. I may prove you wrong. I'm a lot tougher than I look."

"Where is our picnic basket," Cecily called. "I'm thirsty."

While Ryan ran back to the car, Serena sat down next to Cecily to wait for his return. "Thanks for coming."

"I don't know why I'm here," Cecily replied. "I'd much rather be at the pool with the girls. The conditions here are positively primitive. There's sand everywhere. I don't even have a chair or an umbrella. What kind of beach is this?"

"Juni packed pineapple juice and champagne. You can make a drink for yourself. And if you haven't noticed, there are men here. Lots and lots of men." Serena nodded to a pair standing nearby. "Handsome men, with fabulously muscled, gorgeously tanned bodies. I'm sure once I leave you, you'll have plenty of company."

Cecily studied the two men with a keen eye. "They look French. I've never had a French man. They're supposed to be ravenous in bed."

"So I've heard," Serena said.

By the time Ryan returned with the basket, Cecily was pleased with her choice to come and ready to pop the cork on the bottle of champagne. Serena tugged her T-shirt over her head and stepped out of her shorts, then she and Ryan crossed the sand to where he'd left the boards.

"How's she doing?" he asked.

"She's fine. She's got her eye on a couple of surfers. I'm sure she'll have plenty of interesting stories to tell the others when she gets back."

"I'm glad you decided to come," Ryan said.

"Don't be nice to me, Quinn," she teased. "Or we'll start this thing all over again."

"How do you want me to act?" he asked.

His gaze drifted down her body and Serena felt a shiver race through her. She hadn't deliberately chosen a bikini that enhanced her assets but was pleased by his reaction in spite of herself. "Aloof. Indifferent. Like most attractive men."

"What does that mean?"

She smiled coyly. "You know. The way you probably treat every other woman who has crossed your path."

"And how do I treat women?" he asked, picking up one of the longboards from the sand and arranging it next to the other one.

"You're how old?"

"Twenty-eight. How old are you?"

"Twenty-seven." She bent down next to him and idly brushed the sand off the board. "I would have guessed you were a little younger. You look younger. So, you're twenty-eight and you're unmarried."

"And?"

She slowly stood. "In my experience that either means you're gay or that you're a horse's arse to women. It's a simple formula. If you were good to the women in your life, you'd be married by now. Some smart girl would have snatched you up and hauled you to the altar. Tell me I'm right."

He glanced up at her. "It might be a little true," he said with a wry grin. "I don't mean to be an arse. I just haven't found the right woman yet."

"Is there a right woman?"

"I hope so," Ryan murmured. "Maybe not. Maybe I met her already and let her go."

"What do you want from a woman? Maybe we should start there."

Ryan squatted down beside the board and ran his hand along the edge. "I want someone who is witty and clever and spontaneous. Someone who enjoys the outdoors. Someone who is their own person."

"Ah, no clingy types. No whiners or whingers?"

"Exactly," he said.

"And she has to be beautiful and sexy and a tigress in bed. And she has to cook and clean and pick up your dirty knickers, with a smile on her face."

"Exactly," he said.

She wagged her finger at him and grinned. "See? I was right. You are a horse's arse."

"All right, we're here to surf, not to tear my ego to shreds."

On the beach over the next half hour, Ryan did his best to teach her the basics of surfing. When she'd finally mastered the little hop required to get from her belly to her feet, Ryan decided she was ready to try her first wave.

"It's not so hard," she said as they walked to the water's edge.

"You haven't gotten in the water yet." He stopped and stared out at the horizon. "So, we can do this one of two ways. We can paddle out together on the same board, and I can help you get up so you can get a feel for the correct technique. This would require that we touch, though, in a somewhat intimate manner."

"And what's the second choice?"

"I'll swim out behind the board, and I'll give you a shove and off you'll go. You'll do exactly what I instructed you to do, and hopefully, you'll get up. The choice is yours."

"I think I can manage the first option," she said. Serena held up her hand. "I'm wearing my magic ring. It keeps me from feeling any attraction to inappropriate men. Of course, it doesn't work the opposite way."

He ignored her little joke and carried the board into knee-deep water. When she'd stretched out on the board, he lay down behind her, resting between her legs, his head hovering over her backside.

"Well, this is cozy," she said. If Serena thought surfing would be simple, she'd been woefully wrong. She could ignore the attraction she felt to him just by sheer willpower. But she'd been daft to believe that his touch wouldn't affect her. The moment he made contact, her pulse began to race and her breath came in short gasps.

"We can stop. Just say the word."

"I'm fine," she said, trying to sound indifferent.

"Now paddle," he said. "Dig hard. And when a wave comes along, hold tight to the edges of the board."

Serena did as she was told. But it was hard to concentrate with Ryan's body pressed against hers, the sensation sending thrills racing through her. She tried to convince herself that it was the adventure of surfing, but the feel of his chest rubbing up against her thighs was more than she could manage.

To her relief, the ride finally ended and Ryan pushed up, his feet dangling on either side of the board. "You can sit," he said. "I'm going to show you how to pick a wave."

She listened to him as he explained the patterns, letting his voice seduce her into a Zen-like state. In truth, she didn't really care about the surfing anymore. It was just pleasant to spend time with him, to touch him without having to feel guilty and pull away.

"All right," he said. "Here comes a good one. Lie down and paddle, and when I tell you, I want you to get up. I'll keep the board stable as you do. Go, go, go."

Serena set her sights on the shore and dug into the water with her hands. When the board was gliding across the water at a smooth speed, he called out to her and she repeated the movement she'd mastered on the beach. A moment later, he was standing behind her, his hands clasped around her waist.

They rode the wave right onto the beach, and they jumped off the board together. Serena turned and threw her arms around his neck, laughing in delight at her success. He pulled her body against his, into a fierce hug, and picked her up off her feet.

It was such a spontaneous moment that Serena didn't even think about the consequences. But when he finally set her down, she knew something had shifted between them. Ryan reached up and cupped her face in his hand, gazing down into her eyes.

For a long time, they didn't speak, and Serena waited for him to move, holding her breath so long that she had to gasp to draw another. A shiver coursed through her as she smoothed her hands over his chest.

"Tell me not to kiss you," Ryan whispered, desire burning in his eyes.

"Don't kiss me," she said.

"I want to."

"I know. I want you to."

He closed his eyes and tipped his head back as if the effort caused him pain. Slowly, he let his hands drop to his sides, then he turned away from her.

He picked up the board and tucked it under his arm. "I think you're ready to try this on your own."

"I think I'll have to be," she said.

"Go ahead. I'll swim out with you and give you a push."

They spent the rest of the morning trying to forget about that moment on the beach. And when Serena finally gave in to exhaustion, she retreated to Cecily's blanket. Ryan decided to move down the beach to a better break and took the shorter surfboard.

"Where's he going?" Cecily asked.

"To catch some bigger waves," Serena said, wrapping a beach towel around her body.

"Can we go back to the house?"

"In a bit," she said.

"We've been invited out to a club tonight. Those French guys are actually Australian, and they said we should meet them and the rest of their friends at this trendy place. An entire rugby team of hot, horny men. They're playing in some tournament here. We should go."

"You can go," Serena said. "Don't drag me along. I doubt they want to party with an engaged woman. And I don't need a photo of me doing body shots with some randy rugby player."

"But I told them I'd bring you. They both recognized you. They both knew Arabella, too. Apparently her last movie was very big down under. But don't tell her that. She'll be insufferable." Cecily groaned. "Come on, I played nice for you. Now you have to return the favor. You don't have to stay long. Just one drink and you can go."

"All right," she said. "I'll go for a little while."

Cecily wrapped her arm around Serena's shoulder and gave her a hug. "We're going to have fun."

"I hope so."

"You looked great out there," Cecily said. "Adventure guy is a good teacher."

Serena nodded. "Yes, he is. He's a good man."

THE LIGHTS FROM the pool sent wavering shadows into the dark night. The ice in Ryan's drink clinked softly as he took a long sip of Scotch. He glanced at his watch and cursed softly.

Serena and her bridesmaids had left in a white limousine at ten, headed to a nightclub at a luxury resort outside Nadi. They'd been dressed in sexy dresses and heels, in full hair and makeup, ready to seduce any man who looked interesting.

Of course, Miles had accompanied them, hoping to keep the party in hand, but considering Cecily's excitement on the way back from the beach, he'd have his work cut out for him. Her Australian rugby players had agreed to meet them for drinks and dancing and whatever came next.

Serena had promised she'd be back early, but it was nearly two a.m. and Ryan was still waiting. He shouldn't be worried. After all, she'd had a social life long before she'd met him, and that life had included a lot of partying, handsome single men and countless nightclubs. Serena Hightower knew how to handle herself.

That wasn't what was driving him mad. It was all the other thoughts—of Serena enjoying herself, dancing and laughing, kissing other men. He didn't want to feel jealous, and Ryan wasn't convinced that was what it was. It wasn't the men he envied, it was the time they had with her. He and Serena had only a precious few days together, and even an hour or two spent apart seemed like a forever.

He took another sip of his drink and closed his eyes,

picturing her as she'd crawled into the limo. She hadn't even looked like herself. She'd looked like what she really was…a movie star.

Was that why they were called stars? Because they were shiny and beautiful, yet untouchable? Yet he knew a different Serena, a warm, witty, vulnerable woman who wasn't quite sure who she was or where she belonged.

"Here you are. I've been looking all over for you."

Ryan swung his legs off the chaise and stood up, watching as Serena strolled to his spot next to the pool. "You're back," he said.

She'd pulled her hair away from her face and she carried her shoes in her hand. "I've done my duty. I pretended to have a good time, Miles took photos, I danced with my bridesmaids and then spent the rest of the evening fending off the advances of nearly every single man in the club."

She sat down on the end of a wide chaise and then heaved her shoes into the pool. "Good riddance," she muttered.

"You look beautiful," Ryan murmured.

"I hate this dress. It itches. I'd take it off now, but I'm too tired to fetch something else to wear."

Ryan pulled his T-shirt off and held it out to her, then covered his eyes with his other hand. "I promise not to peek."

This time he kept his promise, though the temptation to catch a glimpse of her was nearly overwhelming. But he had to be careful not to court temptation around

Serena. "You can look now." She'd settled herself on the oversize chaise longue and patted the cushion beside her. "Sit," she said.

Ryan glanced over his shoulder at the chaise he'd formerly occupied and weighed the wisdom of returning to that chair. But in the end, he accepted her invitation and stretched out beside her, careful not to make any careless contact.

"Was it any fun at all?" he asked.

"None," she said. "There's no fun in going out anymore. People really don't want me for who I am. They want the movie star. They want the fantasy, especially the men."

"The fantasy?"

She stretched out beside him. "Umm. They usually have a favorite character that I've played. And it doesn't take me long to sort out which one it is. They'll introduce themselves, using their very best come-on, and I can see it in their eyes. They want Frannie or Anna or Laura, not me. And we chat and then I start to notice the disenchantment set in. They begin to realize that I'm not what they thought I was. I'm not clever or flirtatious or ditzy. I'm rather…ordinary. And underneath all this paint, I'm not really that beautiful, either. And then they wander off, disappointed that they didn't get their fantasy and, instead, got stuck with reality."

"I like the reality," Ryan said.

"You've never watched any of my films, so that's all you're left with." She sighed softly. "This is why it's difficult for me to trust people. I wonder if they really hear me or see me—the real me. I'm just an image to them, two-dimensional."

"You must have someone you can trust," he said.

Serena shook her head. "All I am—to any of them—is a paycheck. They don't make money unless I do. And the more I make, the more they make." She glanced over at him. "A few years ago, the director of an independent film gave me a script. I wanted to do it, so I called a meeting to discuss the project with my publicist and my manager and my agent. And by the end of the meeting, they'd convinced me that it was the worst move I could possibly make. I believed them. But when the movie came out, I went to see it, and as I watched another actress do my role, I realized they were wrong. I could have done that role and done it better—if I hadn't let them make my decisions for me."

Ryan saw the regret etched on her pretty face. He couldn't imagine how difficult it must be for her to live in such isolation and yet have everyone in the world know who she was. "What about Ben?" he asked.

"Oh, what about Ben?" she repeated in a wistful voice.

"Can't you trust him?"

"We don't talk about our careers. Not with each other. He's struggled the past few years to find good roles, and it's hard for him to watch me have more success. His ego is a bit bruised."

"So talk to me," Ryan said. "I might not understand, but I'll listen."

She swung her legs off the chaise and stood up. Serena walked to the edge of the pool, then gracefully dove in. Ryan watched her as she swam to the far end, her slender figure distorted by the light from the pool. She broke the surface, her head tipped back, the water running off her in a smooth sheet.

"Come on in," she said.

Ryan walked to the edge, then shook his head. "I think I'll stay here." His fingers twitched as he imagined touching her, imagined stripping the T-shirt from her body and exploring the curves beneath. But he knew it would be good between them, even without the fantasy.

She swam toward him and then bobbed beneath the water right below him. Ryan sat down and kicked his feet in the warm water. Crossing her arms on the pool deck, Serena let her bare legs float out behind her.

"I don't want to tell you all my problems."

"I'm happy to listen."

"I don't think your job description calls for this, though. Adventure guide and amateur therapist?"

Ryan stared out across the swimming pool. "I enjoy getting to know you, Serena. You're a very intriguing person."

Her eyebrow arched. "I am. I was named one of Hollywood's ten most-intriguing people last year. I have no idea what that means. I'd expect it's yet another way to make me into something I'm not."

She pushed away from the edge of the pool and floated out on her back into the middle, the gentle movement of her arms propelling her through the water. Ryan's gaze skimmed along the length of her body, lingering over her breasts. His T-shirt clung to her curves like a second skin, and Ryan found the scene just as tantalizing as if she were swimming naked.

Naked, half-dressed, fully clothed. It didn't matter. He couldn't rid himself of this powerful attraction. She was engaged, her wedding was scheduled, and still, his body hadn't gotten the message. Desire burned deep inside him, and nothing he did seemed to put out the flame. "Tell me about Ben," Ryan said. "How did you meet him?"

"We played opposite each other in a film called *Solstice*," she said, staring up at the night sky. "We had a typical movie-set affair. I fell in love with his character and he fell in love with mine. After the shoot was over, we decided to keep seeing each other. As fate would have it, our schedules lined up, and one thing led to another."

"And you love him?"

"Sometimes, I think I do. And then other times, I'm sure I don't. I'm still not sure who he is."

"I don't understand," Ryan said.

"It's as if we're still playing our parts. We never stopped."

Ryan frowned. "And you're marrying him?"

Her feet dropped into the water and she stood up in the middle of the pool. "Yes. It's all planned."

"But don't you want more?"

"Like what?" Serena asked. "I know we're not going to have a perfect marriage. But who does? I don't expect a fairy tale. I think it's better to be realistic about it all."

"I don't understand. Why are you so willing to settle?"

"I lived through my parents' multiple marriages.

They destroyed each other because they expected so much from the other person. And then they both moved on, still expecting a perfect relationship with the next person. They never found it and they were never happy. So I think it's much better to accept the fact that marriage is never going to be everything you want. You have to learn to accept it for what it is."

In truth, Ryan could see her point. She was walking into this marriage with her eyes wide open. And maybe it would be easier to make it work. But he couldn't help but believe that she deserved more. She deserved a man who didn't need to pretend to make her happy. A man like—

Ryan cursed inwardly. No, not a man like him. As much as he wanted to believe in the fantasy, Serena was right on that count. Though there was an intense attraction between them, there was no future for them.

Serena swam over to the steps and got out of the pool, running her palms over her wet hair as she walked toward him. Ryan reached for a towel from the stack sitting beside him and handed it to her. Serena wrapped it around her, beneath the T-shirt, then slipped the wet shirt over her head. A few seconds later, she skimmed her thong down over her calves and kicked it aside.

Ryan groaned inwardly, imagining the naked body beneath the thick cotton towel. He slowly got to his feet and walked back to the chaise, then sat down. It would take so little to just tug the towel free, to seize the chance to touch her and seduce her, to finally act on the desire that pulsed between them.

Serena sat down next to him, pulling the towel over her bare legs. She drew in a deep breath and sighed. "I love the smell of frangipani."

4

SERENA SIGHED SOFTLY as she curled her body into the warmth. Birds sang on the early morning breeze, the melodies dragging her from slumber. She slowly opened her eyes and found herself staring across the smooth expanse of Ryan's chest. She was tucked against his body, his left arm holding her close. Holding her breath, she tried to move, but the moment she did, Ryan stirred.

She could feel the heat of his skin against hers and realized that the towel she'd wrapped around her body last night was gone. The warmth of him seeped into her limbs, and she enjoyed the sensation for a long moment, drawing her leg up over his.

Squinting at the sky, she tried to determine the time. The girls had probably returned late from their night out and would likely sleep until noon. But there was always a chance they'd come down to the pool to let the sun bake out their hangovers. She'd insisted she hadn't slept with Ryan, but this scene wouldn't do much to confirm that fact.

"Quinn," she whispered. "Quinn, wake up." She smoothed her hand over his chest, then reached up to touch his lips. "Quinn."

His eyelids fluttered, then opened. He met her gaze, his brow etched with confusion. "Hi," he said.

"Good morning."

Ryan slowly sat up, rubbing his eyes. She snatched at the towel and quickly pulled it over herself, but not before he'd caught sight of her naked body. "We—we fell asleep."

"I can see that."

Serena sat up beside him. She wasn't sure what to say. She'd only ever slept with a man after they'd had sex. Her gaze skimmed over his chest and came to rest on the bulge in the front of his shorts. Though she knew his response probably wasn't caused by her presence, she preferred to think that he'd been dreaming about seduction.

Reaching up, Serena tried to run her fingers through the tangles in her hair. Ryan reached out and rearranged a strand that kept falling into her face.

"There. Much better."

"Thanks, Quinn."

"Do you want to try calling me Ryan? Now that we've slept together, I think it would be all right."

"Ryan," she murmured.

He grinned. "Much better."

Serena could imagine what she looked like—wild hair, smudged makeup and an imprint from the chaise cushion impressed into the right side of her face. She wanted to run into the house and make herself presentable, but she couldn't bring herself to leave him.

"How did you sleep?" he asked.

"Really well." Her nights recently had been plagued with restless dreams and frustrating bouts of insomnia. But last night, she'd fallen into a dreamless sleep that had left her perfectly refreshed and ready for another day.

"I'm going to go take a shower and get dressed. Why don't you figure out what we're going to do today."

"With or without the girls?" he asked.

"Without. After all, we just slept side by side, without giving in to temptation, so we've proven we don't need a chaperone. And they're a lost cause in the adventure department. But no matter. We'll have fun on our own." She smiled. "I'll see you in a bit, Ryan."

She liked the sound of his name coming off her lips. It had been easy to keep him at a distance when he'd been just Quinn, the adventure guide. But there was no denying that they'd grown closer over the past couple of days. They'd become friends, and as such, she ought to call him by his first name.

"Ryan," she said to herself as she strolled back to the house.

Serena stepped inside the house and rounded the corner into the kitchen. To her surprise, the girls were gathered around the table, still dressed in their evening clothes and digging into a lavish breakfast that Juni had laid out.

They all looked up at her. She pulled the towel more

tightly around her body, then forced a smile. "What? I just went for an early morning swim."

"What happened to your hair?" Bella asked.

Serena reached up, then cursed softly. "I slept on it when it was wet."

A few seconds later, she heard Ryan come in behind her. He stopped short when he noticed the group gathered at the table. Serena glanced back and saw that he was holding her dress in one hand and her thong in the other.

"Good morning," he said. He quickly gave her her clothes, then continued on through the kitchen and up the back stairs to his room.

"I'm going to grab a shower," she said. "Save some breakfast for me."

She hurried up to her room and shut the door behind her. Closing her eyes, she slumped against the door, letting the towel fall to the ground. Through the walls, she could hear Ryan in the next room, whistling a soft tune.

This was crazy. She wanted to go to him, to fall into his bed and make love for the rest of the day and the night. Since the moment they'd met, she'd felt this undeniable attraction. But after last night, she was forced to realize that this was more than just some silly infatuation.

She was supposed to marry Ben in a matter of weeks, but instead, she wanted to run away with Ryan. With him, she could be entirely herself. For the first time, she felt as if someone understood her and accepted her for the person she'd always been.

And she wanted to explore the feelings she had for

him. There was no doubt that he was attracted to her, as well. She could see it in the way he looked at her, in the way he touched her. Yet he'd respected the boundaries between them, giving her the space to come to a decision on her own. She wanted him, more than any man she'd ever met. But as long as she was engaged to Ben, she couldn't move forward with Ryan.

Her choice was simple. Marry a man she didn't love and avoid a scandal, or call off the wedding, turn her life upside down and possibly ruin her career, for a man she'd just met.

Maybe her reputation was deserved—maybe she was capricious, fickle, unstable.

Serena took a ragged breath. But only she knew what was in her heart, and it was suddenly quite clear. She didn't want to marry Ben. She didn't want to be caught in a marriage that was doomed to fail. Ryan was right. She deserved better.

Serena searched the room for her phone and found it on the bed. Though she had international service, she wasn't sure if that covered Fiji. She set her location, then scrolled through her contacts before pressing the call button.

One of her former costars was a pilot and also a good friend. He'd know how to help her. "Jeff, it's Serena Hightower."

"Serena! How are you? How are the wedding plans going? We had to send our regrets. I'm going to be on location in Toronto that weekend."

"Actually, I need your help. I want to charter a jet to get me from Nadi on Fiji to…" Where could she go to hide? "Auckland," she finally said. "New Zealand. I have no idea how to do it. Can you help me?"

"I have a friend who runs a charter service. He probably has some contacts in that part of the world. When do you want to fly?"

"Tonight," she said. "Late. Midnight or later?"

"I'll see what I can do," Jeff said. "Can I call you back?"

"Yes, thank you," Serena said. "I owe you."

"Well… I've actually got a project I'm hoping to direct. I'd love it if you'd read through the script."

"Send it to me, to my private email. Don't send it through my agent." She gave him her address, then rang off.

Serena set the phone down on the bed and closed her eyes. Was she really prepared to do this? She'd have to call Ben and tell him. But maybe it would be best to wait until later, right before she left the island. She sucked in a sharp breath. Right before *they* left the island. That is, *if* Ryan agreed to come with her, which might not be a given considering all that he had at stake on this trip.

"This is real," she murmured to herself. "This isn't some crazy fantasy. I'm not pretending anymore. This is real."

A soft rap sounded on her bedroom door, and Serena grabbed a robe and wrapped it around her naked body. She pulled the door open, expecting Ryan to be on the other side. But Cecily pushed her way into the room.

"As your maid of honor, I feel duty bound to tell you that I'm so happy you are shagging the pool boy."

"Shh! He's right next door. And I'm not shagging the pool boy. He's not the pool boy."

Cecily waved her hand. "You know who I'm talking about. And I think it's about time you evened the score with Ben. Now everything will be balanced before you get married. He's had his affairs and you'll have had yours."

"Ceci, we're not having an affair. Nothing happened. We fell asleep on the chaise. I went swimming and wrapped myself in a towel and—it was perfectly innocent." She took Cecily's arm and led her to the door, but the other woman dug in her heels.

"Serena, as much as I'm looking forward to standing up with you in that hideous dress that your wedding planner chose, I do want you to be happy. And you need to know something." She paused, then took Serena's hands in hers. "It's not just his costars. Ben tried to hook up with me a few months ago. We were on a red-eye to New York and he invited me to his hotel after we landed."

Serena swallowed hard. "Did you go?"

"Of course not. I turned him down. The point is, he was well aware that I was your maid of honor and he still propositioned me. And when I declined, he came on to one of the flight attendants. I'm not sure if anything happened there, but she seemed interested."

"Thank you for telling me," Serena said.

Cecily smiled. "If you don't shag that pool boy, I may have to." She walked to the door. "It sounds like he's in the shower. Maybe you could go in there and offer to scrub his back."

Serena closed the door behind Cecily. There was no doubt in her mind now, no more waiting. She'd call Ben right now and end it.

Then she'd call Thom Perry and end her career by informing him that the star of his newest film was about to be embroiled in a proper Hollywood scandal.

RYAN AND SERENA had dinner that night at Juni's favorite restaurant, a traditional Fijian place that her sister ran near Lautoka. They'd invited the bridesmaids, but the girls had decided to attend a rugby game and then party with their new friends from Australia. Ryan had been glad for the time alone with Serena.

They'd started with *kokoda,* raw fish marinated in lime juice and seasoned with coconut and tomatoes and chilies. That course was followed up with a delicious prawn curry. And then, the specialty of the restaurant, a *lovo* feast. Endless platters of pork and fish and lamb emerged from the underground pit, the dishes cooked beneath banana leaves until fragrant and tender.

Ryan and Serena ate until they couldn't eat any more, then joined in with the rest of the patrons to celebrate the birthday of one of the chefs. There was dancing and drinking, and when they finally decided to leave, it was nearly midnight.

Ryan held her hand as they walked back to the Jeep. He couldn't remember ever having so much fun on a date—even though this hadn't been a date. He and Serena just seemed to fit, as if they were made to be together. Mal and Rogan had tried to explain that they had something similar with their women, but Ryan had always thought it was lovesick blather. But now he understood exactly what they meant.

"I can't believe how much I ate," she said.

"You do have a good appetite," he said. "But who wouldn't? That food was incredible."

"I've been on a diet for the wedding, but I've decided to give it up."

She'd made several other comments over the course of the evening that had made him think she was reconsidering her plan to get married. Though he didn't want to be the cause of such a major decision, Ryan also didn't want Serena to spend the rest of her life with someone else.

He helped her into the Jeep, then slid in behind the wheel. They drove the winding roads down to the Queen's Highway, then headed back toward Nadi. He glanced over a few times at Serena, but she was staring out the windscreen, her mind somewhere else.

"Are you all right?" he asked.

"Fine," she said.

He wanted to pull the Jeep off the road, yank her into his arms and kiss her, if just to reassure her that she wasn't alone. But their relationship had changed so much in the past couple of days, he wasn't sure where they stood.

By the time they reached the house, Ryan was ready to jump out of his skin. He pulled up to the house, noticing the limo parked outside. The girls had called for the car to take them to the nightclub, but it was far too early for them to be back. Unless something had happened.

He turned off the ignition and gazed at Serena. He

hated feeling like this—uneasy and vulnerable. He circled the Jeep and opened her door. If she had something to say to him, then he needed her to say it. He grabbed her hand and stopped her as she headed for the front door "You want me to leave the island, don't you?"

Serena sucked in a sharp breath and looked around. "How did you know?"

"It doesn't take a mind reader to see you're not happy."

"I'm not," she said. "But I've finally faced the fact that I have to put a stop to this."

"I'm sorry if I put any stress on you. I never meant—"

"We can talk about this later," she said. "Right now you need to pack. The limo is here to take us to the airport. I've hired a private jet."

Ryan frowned. "We? What plane? You want to come with me?"

"No, I want you to come with me," Serena said. "Isn't that what you asked?"

"I asked if you wanted me to leave the isalnd."

"I do. *With me*. We're going to Auckland. Or Phuket. Or Hawaii, or wherever." She shook her head. "You do want to come, don't you?"

Ryan cursed softly. That's what this was about? She was planning her escape? But it wasn't just hers—it was *their* escape. "Yes. Of course," he said, not giving himself a chance to consider the consequences.

"I called Ben to cancel the wedding, but he didn't answer, so I left a message. I know, I know. It's a horrid way to end a relationship. But I didn't want to wait any longer. I'll wait and call Thom from the car because he'll set Miles on our trail. I have no idea if Ben is going to go to the media with this. But hopefully, we'll be off the island by then."

Stunned, Ryan took her hand. "Are you certain you want to do this?"

"Yes. Absolutely. Now we have to pack."

"No," Ryan said, shaking his head. "There's something else we need to do first." He pulled her into his arms, his lips coming down on hers in a desperate kiss. He'd waited so long to kiss her, and it was everything that he'd imagined it would be.

Ryan's arms circled her waist, and her body melted against his, all soft flesh and sweet curves. His hands grasped the silky fabric of her skirt, tugging it up until he could run his palms over her hips, not caring that they were in full view of the waiting driver.

Serena moaned softly and he deepened the kiss, his hands smoothing over her bare backside. When he finally drew away, she was limp in his arms, her fingers clutching at the front of his T-shirt. Her eyes fluttered open and she gazed up at him.

"We have to pack," she said in a shaky voice.

"You chartered a plane? How much did that cost?"

"Enough to put a big dent in my bank card limit. We don't have to go to Auckland. I just figured you'd know somewhere I could hide there. I need to stay off the radar until this all blows over."

"It's all right. We can go to Auckland."

She held out her hand and he laced his fingers through hers. "Are you sure you want to come with me? You're going to get caught up in this mess, and I don't know what they're going to say about you. And this will probably harm your reputation as much as it ruins mine."

"I don't care. This is a much more interesting adventure than I could have ever planned. I'm in new territory here. And I'm not sure I could say goodbye to you."

"All right. But I'm warning you, it'll get really horrid before it gets better. Thom Perry will not be happy."

"I can handle it," Ryan said.

She pushed up on her toes and kissed him softly. "All right, then. We have ten minutes. Be very quiet. I don't want to wake Arthur and Juni. They work for Thom, and I don't want to ask them to lie for us. But I'll leave a note for them, telling them that we've gone so they don't worry."

They hurried up to their rooms. In a matter of a few minutes, Ryan had stuffed his belongings into his duffel and tossed his empty day pack over his shoulder. He knocked softly on Serena's door and she opened it.

He could tell reality had sunk in and she was scared. Her eyes were wide and her color was high and she chewed nervously on her lower lip as she finished packing. She'd brought three bags but was leaving with just one.

"Do you have your passport?" he asked.

She nodded.

"Your phone? Your wallet?"

She cursed softly, then raced around the room, searching for her purse. It was buried in the bed linens, and when she found it, she pulled it over her shoulder.

"All right. That's it. I'm ready." She grabbed a folded paper from her pocket. "Where should I leave this?"

He opened the door, then took her bag. "On the bed."

She placed the note on her pillow, then turned to him.

"Go down the front steps," Ryan said. "I'll go out the rear and meet you at the car."

Serena nodded, then gave him a quick kiss. "This is it. You can still back out."

"Not a chance," Ryan said. "Now go. And don't knock over anything in the dark."

Ryan tiptoed down the rear stairs and came out in the kitchen. He stopped and grabbed a few things from the refrigerator, then turned to find Arthur watching him from the shadows.

"Jaysus, you scared me, Arthur. How long have you been standing there?"

"I heard you come in," Arthur said. "I thought you might want something to eat, but I can see that you have other plans."

"You might as well know. We left a note for you upstairs. Serena and I are leaving. She's called off the wedding."

A slow smile spread across his face. "This is good news. She has chosen you?"

"I think so. I hope so. We're going to Auckland." He paused. "Keep our secret for as long as you can?"

"I'll keep your secret for as long as I can. Now you must leave. I heard Miss Serena go out. She will be waiting."

Ryan nodded. "Thank you, Arthur."

"You are welcome," Arthur said. "Best of luck to you."

Ryan slipped out the back door and circled the house. Serena was waiting in the backseat of the limo, the door open for him.

He threw his luggage in the boot and crawled in beside her. She was staring down at her phone. "It's done," she said as he shut the door. "I told Thom and then hung up. He'll probably ring me back in a second."

As the limo pulled away from the house, Ryan reached out for the switch next to the privacy screen. It slowly rose, cutting them off from the driver's sight.

"What are you doing?" she asked.

He took the phone from her fingers, switched it off and tossed it on the seat of the car. "I thought I might want to kiss you again," Ryan said.

"I can't believe I did this. For the first time in my life, I made an important decision. I never make decisions. My agent, my managers, my directors—everyone else makes my decisions for me." She laughed softly. "I'm proud of myself."

"How do you think Ben will take it?"

"The breakup? Or my running off with you? This isn't going to make him look good in the media. Especially after all those cheating rumors. They're going to say that's why I canceled the wedding."

"Cheating rumors?"

She nodded. "He cheated on me twice last year. Actually, there might have been more, but I only found out about the professional cheats. He doesn't consider it cheating when you sleep with a costar. He calls it part of his process."

"Bloody hell, Serena, why didn't you say something to me about this? I would have told you to dump the guy in a heartbeat. Any bloke who'd cheat on you is a feckin' wanker."

"He *is* a wanker," she said. "I should have realized that sooner."

"I'd say so."

"And what about you, Ryan Quinn? Are you a wanker, too?"

He caught her chin with his thumb and shook his head. "I'm a lot of things, but I'm not a wanker. I promise."

"All right, then. I guess we're in this together for now."

"We've got a half hour to the airport. I think a bit of snogging might be in order."

"I just called off my wedding, dumped my fiancé, trashed my career and all you want to do is snog?"

Now that she put it in those words, he realized he'd been a bit insensitive to her feelings. "Sorry," he said, sliding across the seat to put some distance between them.

"Can we wait?" she said. "Just a bit?"

"Absolutely. That's completely understandable. I'm sorry."

They sat quietly, the silence growing more awkward with every second that passed. He glanced over at her and saw a smile twitching at the corners of her mouth. "Okay, that was long enough."

"What are you doing to me?" he growled, pulling her on top of him.

"How long would you have waited?" she asked, smoothing her fingers over his cheek.

"As long as you needed."

"What I need is for you to kiss me again," Serena said. "Can you do that?"

"I'll do my best."

THE DRIVER DROPPED them off at a small corporate hangar on the outskirts of the Nadi airport. Serena pulled a wad of cash out of her purse and handed it to him, extracting a promise that he would not tell the girls where she'd gone. No doubt Arthur would explain everything to her bridesmaids once he found her note. The driver smiled and nodded his assent.

The spot was deserted when they got out and Ryan piled their bags near the locked door. They sat down on a nearby bench and he slipped his arm around her shoulders. "You all right?" he asked.

"Yes," she said. "Just a bit numb. And worried that this is going to be a lot worse than I've been expecting."

"How is that?"

"We were due to start the publicity tour for the film the day after our wedding. First L.A., then New York, then London." She glanced over at him. "I'm still going to have to do the tour. It's part of my contract. Unless they split us up, I'm going to have to do it with him."

He stared at her for a long moment, stunned by her admission. "I don't understand. Why would he—? He's in the movie, too?"

"Yes."

"You're not afraid that he'd—"

"No! Ben can get really angry, but he's never been violent." She sighed. "To be honest, I'm really not sure he wanted to get married, either. I think he might be perfectly happy that I called it off."

"Perhaps he will."

Serena drew a deep breath and sighed softly. "I've done a lot of stupid things in my life. But the last few years, I've begun to put things in order. I thought getting married was part of that."

He turned up her face to meet his gaze. "If it wasn't right, you were better off walking away. Don't you want to be certain?"

"How can anyone be certain? Do you think all those couples who ended up divorced weren't certain on their wedding day? Feelings change. People change. My parents have seven marriages between them. They can't seem to get it right, though they sure keep trying." She grabbed his hand and laced her fingers through his. "Someday, maybe I'll get it right."

"You will," he assured her.

She leaned her head against his shoulder and he pulled her closer. Though she'd known him only a few days, she felt as though they'd been best friends forever.

She didn't need to be frightened; she'd made the right choice. Ryan had told her as much and he was solid and sensible.

How long had it been since she could truly trust someone? Everyone she knew had an agenda. Even Ben, the man who was supposed to love her, had managed to profit from their alliance. Photographers had been much more interested in him when he was with her. He'd often been sent projects with the hope of getting them both involved. And while his career had faded slightly over the past few years, hers had only grown.

So what did Ryan want? He wasn't the type who seemed impressed with celebrity. In truth, she was afraid he might find it tedious after a very short time. He didn't understand her career. He'd never seen her movies and would probably be uncomfortable at a Hollywood event. "A bird could love a fish, but where would they live?" she said softly.

He kissed the top of her head. "What?"

"Nothing. It's just a quote from a movie. I can't re-member which one." She couldn't hope for a future with Ryan. In fact she would probably pass in and out of his life without much notice. But she would never forget what he'd done for her, how he'd made her face a deci-sion she'd avoided for so long.

It would be easy to fall in love with him. He was ev-erything she wanted in a man. But it was time to put herself first and stop looking for security in a relation-ship. She needed to make her own decisions.

"How long do you think it will be before they real-ize we're missing?" she asked.

"Arthur already knows. He caught me in the kitchen, but he promised not to say anything until we're well away. As for the girls, they could probably go a day or two before they realize you're gone."

"In my note, I asked Arthur to explain everything

to them, just so they're reassured I wasn't kidnapped by pirates."

"Good idea," Ryan said. "Are you hungry?"

"I am. But where are we going to get anything to eat?"

He picked up his day pack and unzipped it, then pulled out a bottle of champagne. "It's still cold. I figured we had something to celebrate."

"Do you have anything to eat in there?"

"I do. Some fruit and some of Juni's prawn curry. I didn't grab utensils, though, or glasses. We'll have to eat with our fingers and drink out of the bottle."

Serena had never met a man quite like Ryan. Most of the men she'd been with had been self-centered and egotistical. They'd treated her more like an accessory than an equal partner in the relationship. But Ryan was always looking out for her, making sure she was comfortable and safe.

It's the little things, she thought to herself as she watched him open the bottle of champagne. He'd helped her up the cliff, holding her hand when the footing grew steep or slippery. He'd shown her how to surf and helped her escape. And now he'd been smart enough to bring food.

"You're going to make some woman a wonderful husband," she said as he handed her the champagne.

"I don't know about that. I'm not cut out for that kind of life."

"But look at how good you are to me."

"That's easy. You're my client."

Serena frowned. "You wouldn't be good to me if I wasn't your client?"

"No, of course I would be. It's just, when I'm with you, I'm in guide mode. I want to make sure you enjoy yourself."

"Well, you're officially no longer my guide," she said. "You're fired. Now you can treat me the way you treat all the other women in your life."

"You make it sound as if there are a lot of them."

Serena took a sip of the champagne, then coughed as the bubbles went up her nose. "There aren't?"

"No. I have a small group of friends who are girls. But I'm not in a relationship with any of them."

"Oh, so you're friends with benefits?" she asked.

"Yes. I guess that's what you'd call it. The women are kind of spread out all over the world, mostly in the places where I guide trips. I don't have much time to devote to a real relationship, so whenever I'm in town, we just...you know."

"Hook up," she said.

"Yes," Ryan replied.

"So you're a man-slut," she said.

"No. I don't take advantage. It's a mutual thing." He grabbed the champagne bottle and took a drink. "No one wants a guy who's never around."

"Same thing with actresses. We're almost as bad as musicians. But it's harder for us to do the friends-with-benefits thing since there's always the worry of a sex tape or the tabloid tell-all. We have to be much more cautious."

"I'm not the kind of guy to kiss and tell," he said.

"I realize that. I know I can trust you."

Ryan's mobile rang and he pulled it out of his pocket. Thom Perry's name came up on the screen and he turned and showed it to Serena.

"Do you think he's figured out I'm with you?" she asked.

"Yes. He wouldn't be calling at one a.m. if it wasn't an emergency."

"Are you going to answer it?"

"No, I'll wait and call him back once we're in the air."

They finished off the prawn curry, and after that, the champagne. A soft rain had begun to fall and they huddled under the small roof above the hangar door.

By the time the plane rolled up a half hour later, the drizzle had become a downpour and they were both in a buoyant mood.

Serena stood up and walked out onto the tarmac, turning her face up to the sky. The droplets were warm and soothing. It was as if the rain could wash away all the mistakes she'd made. Her life started now, at this perfect moment.

Ryan joined her and slipped his arms around her waist before capturing her lips in a long, delicious kiss. For the first time in her life, she had everything she could possibly want. She was happy and carefree and caught up in a wonderful romance.

Serena didn't care about the future. For now she was happy to live in the present—as long as that present included Ryan.

He drew back and smiled down at her, wiping the

rain from her cheeks. Then he looked over his shoulder. "Our ride is here," he said.

The door to the jet dropped open and Ryan jogged to the hangar to grab their bags. Then he held out his hand to her. "Come on. Let's get out of here."

Serena wasn't sure how this would work out, or whether she'd regret walking away from her wedding. She wasn't sure how she felt about Ryan or how he felt about her. But all that mattered was that right now she was completely free and ready to see what the future held.

5

AFTER A QUICK VISIT from a sleepy customs agent, the Learjet took off in the rain, then turned southwest and set a course for Auckland. It was the beginning of a new day, but for Ryan, that day brought a host of complications.

He'd made a promise to Thom Perry that he'd do this job, and now he was in the middle of a mess that was going to cost his "boss" a lot of money. It would cost him his big payday, too. The surf school would be on hold for a few more years.

Ryan knew what he ought to do—call Thom and give him an update on the situation. Disappearing into the night without a trace would only cause more problems. Yet he didn't want to break Serena's trust. Somewhere along the way, his loyalties had shifted from Perry to Serena. But was he letting his attraction to her color his decisions? He'd all but told her to break up with her fiancé, and now that she had, he was beginning to wonder if he'd made a mistake.

He'd acted out of purely selfish desires. He wanted Serena and he couldn't have her as long as she was attached to another man. So he'd waited, allowing the desire between them to smolder, waiting for her to make the decision. But what if she really did belong with Ben Thayer, and what if Ryan had ruined any chance she had for happiness?

He sank back into the wide leather seat and closed his eyes. Wasn't this always the way it worked for him? He never let himself get too close to a woman. But there was something different with Serena. Maybe it was the thrill of seducing a celebrity. Or perhaps there were real emotions between them. Having never experienced either, he wasn't sure he could recognize the difference.

"I found the whiskey," Serena said, sitting down next to him and tucking her bare feet underneath her. She'd changed out of her wet clothes into a faded T-shirt and a pair of yoga pants. She'd wrapped a towel around her wet hair and had washed off the makeup she'd worn on their date. She looked…beautiful.

She set a glass down in front of him and filled it half-full.

"Isn't this where we started?" he asked, reaching out to pick up the glass.

"I think it was," Serena said. "And I remember this." Leaning close, she brushed her lips against his. "Yes, I remember that. But we didn't finish what we started then."

She smiled coyly at him, then took his drink and set it on the table beside his seat. "As I recall, this is what I wanted to do next." Serena reached down for the hem of her T-shirt, then slowly pulled it over her head. Ryan's breath caught in his throat as she straddled his legs.

"This is what you had in mind?"

"In my dreams, anyway," she murmured. Her arms rested on his shoulders and she began to tease at his mouth, kissing and nibbling. Ryan groaned, pulling her into a deep kiss, his palms skimming over her naked back.

Her skin was like warm silk, and he wanted to take his time and explore what she offered. But they'd been waiting so long to indulge their desire that neither one of them wanted to slow down.

Serena reached for the buttons of his shirt and undid them, kissing a path along the skin she exposed. He tossed aside the towel that covered her damp hair and twisted his fingers through the strands at her nape. Wave after wave of sensation raced through his body, and Ryan closed his eyes and tried to maintain control.

It had been a while since he'd been with a woman. Back-to-back guiding trips hadn't left him much of a chance to take care of his sexual needs. But even in his wildest fantasies, he'd never imagined that his trip to Fiji would take this turn.

He pulled her body against his, his lips finding the taut peak of her nipple. A soft sigh slipped from her throat as he drew her flesh into his mouth. The scent of her skin was intoxicating, and when he moved to her neck, the intensity increased. The mix of floral and citrus scents filled his head, every sense in his body coming alive.

He couldn't seem to process it all, and Ryan tried to

think rationally. But he was operating on pure instinct, driven by his desire and his need to possess her.

She crawled off his lap and kneeled at his feet, reaching for the button on his shorts. Just the thought of her lips and tongue on his shaft was enough to shatter his control. But he wouldn't allow the pleasure to be one-sided during the first experience between them.

Ryan drew her to her feet and peeled the yoga pants down her hips. She wore a scrap of a thong beneath and he hooked his finger into the side strap and tugged her closer.

He pressed his mouth to her belly, and Serena leaned into him, her arms wrapped around his neck. Her stomach was flat and finely muscled, and he splayed his fingers over her backside, drawing her closer as his kisses dipped lower.

Ryan measured his breathing, consciously trying to slow the pace of his seduction, but he was dancing on the edge. He wanted to throw her down onto the seat and bury himself inside her. Instead, he focused on her pleasure, drawing the thong down to her ankles. She kicked it off but then pulled away from him before he could take his first taste.

Ryan got up and knelt on the seat, watching her walk down the aisle naked. She opened the door to the bathroom and stepped inside, then emerged a few seconds later with a box of condoms. Ryan gasped. "They stock condoms on this plane?"

She shook her head. "I asked for them when I chartered the jet."

"You requested condoms?"

"It's not unusual. I figured we might need them. And we do."

"The pilot knows we're doing this?"

She pointed to a small plastic bubble on the bulkhead. "That's a camera, and I'm pretty sure he can watch if he wants. Let's give him a good show."

She pulled him to his feet and stripped off his shirt and shorts. His boxers followed, and when the clothes were kicked aside, she tore a condom from the package and deftly sheathed him.

Ryan held his breath as her fingers danced over his stiff shaft. The thought that someone might be watching made the encounter even more intensely exciting. A tremor raced through his body, and he sucked in a slow, deep gulp of oxygen. Serena looked up at him, then pressed her palm against his chest, gently pushing him down onto his seat.

When he'd settled into the soft leather, Serena straddled his hips and positioned his shaft at the damp spot between her legs. She waited, watching him, her fingers skimming over his brow and lips. And then she bent close and kissed him, sinking down on top of him as the kiss intensified.

He'd never felt anything quite so exquisite as the sensation of penetrating her warmth. Combined with the kiss, it sent a surge of desire pulsing through his body. He circled his arm around her waist, and Serena leaned back, offering him a view of her body as she moved on top of him.

Ryan cupped her breast in his palm, then drew her nipple into his mouth. She moaned softly as she increased her pace, bringing him close to his release. He grasped her hips, slowing things down.

Serena read his cues perfectly. But when she stopped, he glanced up at her. Smiling, she smoothed her palm over her breast, then down her belly until she was touching herself.

The sight of her, so free, her need so raw, was impossibly electrifying. Her eyes were closed, her head tipped back. He waited for her to be ready, and when she began to move again, Ryan knew she was on the edge. He grabbed her waist and rolled her beneath him, seizing control but keeping the pace. Her orgasm was powerful, shaking her body and causing her to cry out in pleasure. Ryan followed her a few seconds later, driving into her warmth before the spasms rendered him breathless and completely spent.

When he'd recovered, Ryan pushed up on his hands and glanced at the camera. "Should we take a bow?" he asked.

Serena giggled. "I lied. That's not a camera," she said. "But your performance does deserve a bow. And an encore."

THE SMALL COTTAGE on the beach was dark and silent when Serena opened her eyes. She stretched her arms over her head, then rolled over. Ryan was lying beside her, his long legs tangled in the sheets, his pillow pulled over his eyes.

She gently pulled the pillow away and smiled as his eyes opened sleepily. "Hello," she said.

"Hi." He reached out and touched her face, and she pressed his hand to her cheek. "Just checking."

"What?" she asked.

"To make sure this wasn't a dream."

Serena brushed her lips against his. "Nope, I'm real."

"Good. I like having you real and in my bed."

She snuggled closer and took a ragged breath. "I'm feeling very real right now. Ryan, I think I've made a mess of this. I don't know that I'm going to be able to go back. Or if they'll want me back."

"That's not going to happen," Ryan said. "You're beautiful and talented and—"

"Sometimes it's not about talent," she said. "It's about playing the game by the rules. And I haven't done that. Canceling the wedding isn't going to help my reputation."

"You'll get through it," he said.

"But maybe not unscathed."

"So, what if you never went back? Could you give it up?"

She thought about his question for a long moment. "I could. I'm not certain I want to, though. It's the only thing I do well. I'm a good actress. I just want to be a good actress on my own terms."

"You've already taken control of your life. Everything is going to be fine, Serena."

She nodded. "And if it isn't, I'll just give it all up. Maybe that's what I ought to do anyway. I can start a new life. Try to live like normal people do, people who have real jobs and real problems. Do you know what kind of problems I have?"

"Tell me," Ryan said, rolling onto his stomach.

"I spent days before this trip trying to decide whether to cut my hair. You have no idea what a momentous decision it was. How many people it might impact. You're trying to decide whether to climb the highest mountain in the world to see where your father died, and I'm paralyzed about whether I should cut my hair. My life is…silly."

He dropped a kiss on her lips. "Do you really want a serious life?"

"Yes. For the first time, I feel like I'm not pretending. I feel like I'm the one in control. And I'm so excited I could scream it to the heavens."

"So, what's the first thing you want to do in your new life?" Ryan asked.

She drew a deep breath. "Right now I could really go for a big, fat-filled meal. Since I've decided to go off my diet, I fully intend to put on fifteen pounds. And I plan to do it as fast as possible. Hamburgers and ice cream shakes and piles of French fries."

Ryan grinned. "Yum. More of you to snog," he teased, nuzzling his face into her naked breast.

She sat up and raked her hair out of her eyes. "What do you have in this place to eat?"

"Not much. I can go fetch takeaway."

"I can cook," she said. "I'm actually quite good at it." Serena jumped out of bed. Tossing her tangled hair over her shoulder, she walked out of the bedroom.

His *bach,* as he called the cottage, was rustic but cozy. Though it didn't overlook the water, it was surrounded by a thick grove of trees, which gave them enough privacy that they could keep all the windows open. The sound of the surf in the distance came in on the breeze and she drew a deep breath of the salt-tinged air.

She hadn't felt so relaxed, so completely carefree, in years. She didn't have to play a part, didn't have to temper what she said or did, didn't have to keep watch for photographers. Here, with Ryan, she was safe to be herself.

Serena pulled open the refrigerator and examined the contents inside. A few moments later, he came up behind her and joined her search. "I told you. Not much to work with. Beer, moldy bread, mustard and Marmite."

Serena pushed back against him, rubbing against his crotch. He was already aroused and she decided that she might not be as hungry as she thought she was.

As she turned to face him, he hooked his hands around her waist, pulling her body fully up against his. His palms smoothed over her belly and she sighed, arching against him. "What are you about?" she murmured.

"I want to enjoy this," he said, his touch drifting down to the damp spot between her legs. "I've never had a naked woman in my kitchen."

"Never?"

Ryan shook his head. "You're the first woman I've ever brought to the *bach*. I usually do my...seducing away from home."

Serena reached up and ran her fingers through his hair as he continued to move against her, his erection growing. "So, either we get takeaway or I send you to the market. What do you have a taste for?"

He grasped her waist and pushed her against the counter, bracing his hands on either side of her. "I love the taste of you," Ryan said, pressing his mouth to her shoulder. "And the smell of you," he continued, drawing a deep breath. Meeting her gaze, he cupped her breast. "And the feel of you. And I could listen to your voice all day long."

"I'm just a feast for the senses," she said.

"A feast," he repeated. He lifted her up onto the counter, then gently parted her legs. "I just need a taste. Just one."

Serena smiled as his tongue found the center of her pleasure. He seemed to exist to make her happy, and yet she still wasn't sure how she felt about him. There was affection and attraction, but he existed in the real world, where a future between them was impossible.

Sex with Ryan was about pleasure and release and not about complicated emotions. That's what she needed right now, a man who didn't demand anything from her. She was exhausted from always trying to please the people in her life, to meet expectations and to put her own desires aside for the good of her "career." Now Serena was going to please herself.

She leaned back and closed her eyes, focusing on the knot of anticipation growing at her core. A wave of exquisite bliss washed over her, her nerves tingling and her toes curling. The impulse to surrender was strong, but Serena fought it, wanting the moment to last longer.

He'd become a student of her responses, and before long, he was taking her on a wild ride, racing her toward the edge, then pulling her back just in time. Serena arched against him, whispering her need, urging him to finish with her and end the lovely torment.

And then, without warning, it hit her. Her body shuddered, and she cried out as the spasms took her over the edge. She'd never experienced an orgasm quite so powerful, and Serena tried to stay aware of everything that he was doing to her. But she lost herself, drowning in a whirlpool of sensation.

When she finally came back to the surface, she was still gasping for breath. Her heart was slamming against her rib cage, and her fingers and toes tingled. "I can't move," she said.

"I suppose I could just leave you here while I go to the market."

She groaned as she sat up. "You are a cruel man," Serena teased. "And I wouldn't go out of the house with that." She glanced down at the erection rubbing against his belly. "I could fix it for you." She wrapped her fingers around his shaft and began to stroke. "It won't take any time at all."

"You are a cruel woman," he countered. "I wager I could last longer than you."

A sound at the front door caught their attention, and he pressed his finger to her lips. A moment later, the door squeaked, and Ryan grabbed Serena and pulled her toward the bedroom.

"Hello?" a female voice called.

He closed the bedroom door behind them and searched the room until he found the board shorts she'd taken off him earlier.

"Stay here," he said.

"Who is that?" she whispered. "Oh God, don't tell me you're married. If you're married, I will kill you."

"It's my sister, Dana. My entire family has keys to this place."

"I thought you lived here alone."

"I do. Now," he said, pulling the board shorts on. He looked down at his lap and cursed at his erection.

"Here, use this," Serena said, tossing him a T-shirt.

"Is anyone here?" Dana called.

Ryan opened the bedroom door and stepped out. "What the hell are you doing here?"

"I could ask you the same thing," Dana cried. "I saw the lights on, and I was afraid someone had broken in. You're supposed to be in Fiji. When did you get back?"

"This morning."

Serena searched for something to put on as she listened to their conversation. She pulled a sundress from her bag and slipped it over her head, covering her naked body.

"What happened? Did you get fired? Did you break the rule? Oh, bloody hell, Mal will pitch a fit."

"I didn't break any rules," Ryan said, closing the door behind him. Their voices grew muffled and she hurried to the door.

"They just didn't need me anymore," Ryan explained. "The girls didn't want an adventure. All they wanted to do was lie about and get a suntan."

Serena pulled the bedroom door open and stepped out. "Actually, I wanted an adventure, but none of my bridesmaids did."

Dana's eyes went wide and her jaw dropped. "But you're—"

Serena crossed the room, holding out her hand. "Serena. And you're Dana. Ryan has told me so much about you. It's a pleasure to meet you at last." She glanced back at Ryan. "What rule did you break?"

"The—the rule to—to get the job done!" Dana said, a bright smile on her face. "It's so nice to meet you. I love your films. Crikey, you're so tiny. I thought you'd be taller."

"I get that a lot. It's probably because most of my costars have been short."

"So, as you can see, nobody broke in, Dana," Ryan interrupted. "Can you go now, please?"

"Oh, I also came to get the coffeemaker. The one at the office broke and we didn't have the money for a new one and you're never home, so I just thought I'd come by and nick yours. I'll just get it and go."

"And what if I want a cup of coffee?" Ryan asked.

She froze. "Oh, yes. I'm sorry. Of course. Then, I'll leave it." Dana glanced over at Serena. "It was a pleasure to meet you. I hope we see each other again."

"I'm sure we will," Serena said.

Dana hurried to the front door, and a few seconds later, it slammed behind her. Ryan released a long breath. "My sister."

"She's lovely," Serena said, turning to face him. "What rule was she talking about?"

"She told you. To get the job—"

"Oh, please. That's bollocks. She's a dreadful liar. And so are you."

He sighed. "My brothers and I have an unwritten rule. No shagging the clients." She opened her mouth to reply, but he held up his hand to stop her. "You should know that Amy, Mal's fiancée, was a client. And Claudia, Rogan's fiancée, was also a client. So the rule has been broken by both of my brothers before I broke it."

"Well, that excuses you, then," she said.

He observed her silently, as if trying to gauge her mood. "You're...angry?"

"No," Serena said. "Actually, I am quite pleased that you decided to break your rule for me. Please say that I was your first."

"You were," he said. "And technically, you weren't my client because you'd fired me."

She nodded. "All right." Serena walked up to him and grabbed the waistband of his shorts, dragging him along to the bedroom. "I think we need to finish what we were doing when your sister arrived."

RYAN OPENED THE front door of the cottage and stepped inside, the sack of takeaway clutched in his hand. "Serena?"

"I'm out here," she called.

He smiled to himself. They'd arrived just that morning and already he'd grown accustomed to having her around. He enjoyed seeing her curled up on his sofa reading a book or standing at the sink getting a glass of water. He liked finding her clothes mixed in with his and smelling her perfume on his pillow. It gave him a surge of satisfaction to walk in the door and call her name and then have her answer.

Ryan set the food on the counter, then wandered through the cottage. He found Serena sitting on the back deck, her feet tucked up under her, his fleece jacket draped around her shoulders. She wore her glasses, making her look more like a schoolteacher than a movie star.

"What are you doing?"

She held up a spiral-bound sheaf of papers. "Reading a script."

"For what?"

Serena shrugged. "It's an independent film. I've been wanting to try something new but—" She stopped short, then closed the script and tossed it on the table. "I'm not even sure they'd want me anymore."

"Of course they would. What does that mean, independent?"

"It's not a studio film. Lower budget, a subject that might not appeal to a broad audience. Quirky, edgy, weird."

"Why would you want to do a film like that?"

"They're usually made quickly, and the character could be interesting or a challenge. It might allow me to stretch as an actor. If I'm going to act, I want to do it well."

"If?"

"I'm thinking maybe I could give it up."

"But if you don't act, what are you going to do?" Ryan asked.

"Well, when I was a little girl, I wanted to be a princess. I have experience. I played a princess in a film. I even have my own tiara."

He wished he'd watched some of her movies before he'd met her. "We don't have our own royal family here in New Zealand, so I'm not sure princess would be a practical choice. What do you enjoy doing? Do you have any hobbies?"

"I like to play with my dogs. And read. I'm pretty good at cooking and baking. I pretend that I garden, though I don't really like getting my hands dirty. So in truth, I know nothing that prepares me for a real job in the real world." She sighed. "I'll figure it out."

Ryan knew he shouldn't expect her to stay in New Zealand for the rest of her life. She had a career that she'd spent years building and a talent that defined her success. Pursuing anything other than acting would be a waste of time. Besides, where else could she make a million dollars for just a few months' work? Certainly not in Raglan. "You're a splendid actress. Maybe you ought to stick with that."

"And what do you want to do when you grow up?" she asked.

"I haven't quite sorted that out yet," he said. "I'm really not free to pursue another career right now."

"But if you were?"

He didn't want to talk about the surf school. It was a dream that probably never would become a reality. He'd hoped to put away the money from the Fiji trip to start his savings. But he wouldn't get anything from Thom Perry now.

He wondered what it felt like to have enough money to buy nearly anything a person wanted. He was always scraping to pay this bill or that one. And even if he did open a surf school, it wasn't the kind of career that would make him a millionaire. That kind of money was made by men far more educated and driven than he was.

"I think I'd be a very fine prince, too."

"Oh," she said. "We could start our own royal family."

"We can shop for proper crowns and robes tomorrow," Ryan said. "I bought dinner. Would you prefer to eat out here or inside?"

"Here would be lovely," she said.

Ryan fetched the dinner and set it up on the table, scooping the pasta into a shallow bowl before handing it to Serena. "I haven't had pasta in ages," she said. "Carbs were forbidden by my trainer and my nutritionist."

"You have a trainer and a nutritionist?" he asked.

"I have an agent, two managers, a publicist, a trainer, a stylist, a makeup artist, a hairdresser, a driver, a housekeeper, a gardener, a pool man, a nutritionist, a manicurist, an aesthetician, an acupuncturist and a therapist. I employ a small army of people to keep me functioning."

"So should I expect you to fall apart completely, now that you don't have them with you?" Ryan asked.

"You'll notice I didn't list boy toy. I'm auditioning you for that role," she teased, pointing at him with her fork.

Ryan smiled, but he had to wonder how she saw him. Was he just a guy who pleased her in bed? Or did she see him as the kind of man she might make a life with? He couldn't seem to get himself past the disparity in their financial situations.

Were there men who could bury their egos so deeply that it didn't make a difference? But if she had millions, then what could he possibly offer her? Anything he wanted to provide, she could purchase on her own. A car, a house, a holiday in some exotic location.

And yet this was the reality of who they were. If he wanted her, he'd have to accept the fact that she had more money than he could ever hope to earn. Ryan cursed inwardly. Perhaps he should stop jumping ahead. He'd never wanted to be responsible for someone's happiness and security. He was happy on his own. What difference did her money make?

"Is boy toy a paid position?" he asked.

"Oh, now we get to it. You want to negotiate?"

"What do boy toys usually make?" Ryan asked.

"It depends what your job responsibilities are. What are you going to give me?"

What could he give her? Ryan wondered. "Complete and utter sexual satisfaction."

"That's all?" she asked.

"Isn't that enough?"

She stood up and circled the table, then crawled onto his lap and wrapped her arms around his neck. "Maybe it is. Actually, I'm sure it is." She kissed him, her lips soft and tasting of tomato sauce. "Does it bother you?"

"The fact that I'm just a sexual object to you?"

"No. The money. Sometimes—actually, most of the time, men find it uncomfortable that I make more than they do. The good men, anyway. Some men can hardly wait to start spending my money. They're the ones I have to avoid."

"No," he lied. "It doesn't make a difference."

"Good. Because you know, it's not as if it's real money."

"It's not? What is it?"

"It's fantasy money," she explained. "I don't earn it. Nothing I do is worth what I earn. I'd do the exact same job for much less. My agent would kill me if he heard me say that out loud." She paused. "I'm not explaining this very well. Do you gamble? I mean, have you ever made money on a bet?"

"I've played poker."

"How much did you win?"

"A couple of hundred."

"Did you feel like you earned that money? It was lucky money, right? And that's what they give me. I'm lucky to be able to do what I do and get paid for it."

In truth, he did understand what she was trying to say. Ryan wasn't sure it made a difference, but it was something to consider. "So my pay as a boy toy is lucky money, too?"

"Yes. It's money you're making for getting lucky. It's the epitome of lucky money."

Ryan laughed, then pushed her off his lap. "Finish your pasta." He reached across the table and grabbed a bread stick from the bag. "You're going to need a big meal. I'm planning to get very lucky tonight."

They finished their dinner, then walked down to the beach to wait for the sunset. They'd spent their first day together, and it had gone better than he'd ever expected.

She slipped her arm through his and rested her head

against his shoulder. "So, what's on the itinerary for tomorrow?"

"What would you like to do?"

"Maybe go into town," she said. "Walk around and see what…where are we again?"

"Raglan," he said.

"See what Raglan has to offer."

"It's not L.A.," Ryan said.

"I don't want L.A.," she said.

"I should stop in at the office," he said. "Face the music. No doubt Dana has spread the tale of what she saw earlier this morning. Don't worry. She's discreet. She'll just tell my brothers and my mother."

"Your mother?"

"She'll be thrilled," Ryan said.

"That you have a girlfriend?"

"Is that what you are? My girlfriend?" Ryan asked.

"Sure. I could be your girlfriend."

"You have a boy toy and I've got a girlfriend. I'd say we're making progress here."

But progress *to what* was the real question.

6

"I'LL BE FINE," she said. "I have my hat and my sunglasses, and no one will recognize me," Serena said. "I just want to pick up a few things and then I'll walk back to your place."

Ryan looked out the windscreen. They were parked on the main street of Raglan, a half-hour walk from the beach house. "But I can come with you. You know what will happen if someone recognizes you."

Serena had been in New Zealand for only a day but she'd already grown restless hanging about the *bach*. She'd made elaborate plans to spend her day at the most important spots in Raglan—the market, the bakery and the hardware store.

News of her canceled wedding hadn't hit the media yet, so Serena assumed Ben and Thom had talked and decided to keep the news to themselves. They were no doubt hoping to get her back to Los Angeles and down the aisle before anyone was the wiser.

"I just need a little more time to work out what I'm

going to say to everyone." She paused. "Has Thom rung you this morning?"

Ryan pulled his phone out of his pocket and rolled through the incoming calls. "Yeah. Six—no, seven—times since we left Fiji. Has he rung you?"

"I haven't turned my phone on. I'm just going to leave it off until I've decided what to say. Are you going to call Thom back?"

"Not until you do," Ryan said.

"Good. We should both be on the same page. You don't think they assume I broke my engagement because I'm having an affair with you, do you?"

"I don't know," Ryan said, confused by her question.

"That would be bad. I don't want to look like a slut. Or a cheat. But if Ben calls me a cheat, then I'll have to reveal to everyone that he cheated on me first." She paused. "He probably knows that's what I'd do. No, he won't say I cheated." She groaned, pressing her hands to her head. "This is why I can't think about this now." She leaned over and kissed his cheek. "I have to go."

"You know how to get home? Just follow Wainui Road and it will take you all the way to the *bach*. It's about two kilometers."

She tugged on her hat and slipped her sunglasses on. "That's brilliant. A proper stroll. And I have my phone and my wallet and passport if I get lost. I'll be fine. I've driven in L.A. I can certainly navigate a small village like this."

"All right." He pulled her into a hug. "I'm just going to check into the office and then I'll stop and grab some groceries. I won't be gone more than a couple of hours."

She jumped out of the Range Rover. "I'll see you later." Serena pushed the cap down on her head and crossed the street.

RYAN WATCHED UNTIL Serena disappeared into the local pharmacy.

He thought about waiting for her, just to make sure she didn't have any problems. But then he realized that Serena had just discovered her independence. She wasn't helpless and she didn't need him hovering over her.

Ryan threw the Range Rover into gear and turned the truck toward the office. Though Dana wasn't normally a gossip, he wanted to talk to her before she spread tales throughout the family about Ryan's new houseguest.

When he pulled into the car park at Max Adrenaline, he recognized all three cars. Dana, Mal and Rogan were in the office. "Bloody hell," Ryan murmured. Maybe he ought to just go home. But he'd have to face them sooner or later. And it was better to do it now before they had a chance to speculate.

He switched off the ignition and hopped out of the truck. Duffy was lying on the porch and perked up as Ryan passed, his tail thumping on the plank floor. "Hey, Duff." He reached down and gave the dog a pat. Duffy got to his feet and followed Ryan through the screened door.

He found his three siblings in the workroom. They were going over gear for an upcoming trip, sorting through the ropes and harnesses and hardware, checking for any damage.

They watched him silently as he walked over to the brand new coffeepot and poured himself a cup. Ryan glanced around the room. "Go ahead. Have at it. I'm ready for the worst of it."

"What the hell were you thinking?"

"Did you sleep with her?"

"Jaysus, Ryan, when you break the rules, you do it up right."

The comments tumbled over each other until he held up his hand to silence the critics. "All right. Now that you've had your say, I'll have mine. Serena is going to be staying with me until she sorts out what she wants to do. Yes, we are…involved, but nothing happened until after she broke off her engagement. I was not the cause of that. There were other factors at work. Although meeting me might have pushed her toward that decision a bit quicker, I'm sure she would have canceled the wedding anyway. And no, we won't be making our fee on this trip. So we'll have to make that money up elsewhere."

Mal sat down, running his hands through his hair. "You couldn't have convinced her to stay for the entire week? That was a lot of money to just toss away."

Ryan shrugged. "It was my money. My choice. And there's nothing I can do about it now."

"Rogan told me you considered this a freelance job," Mal said.

"There is something you can do," Dana said. "Thom Perry called this morning. He wants you to call him."

"I'm not going to do that."

"He said that if you deliver Serena Hightower to Los

Angeles by the end of the week, he'll double your fee. And he'll triple it if you convince her to go through with the wedding."

"Did you tell him we were here in Raglan?"

"No," Dana said. "But I promised that I'd relay his message if you called in."

He smiled at his sister. "Thank you," he murmured. His siblings observed him silently. "What? You can't believe I'd take his offer. I'd be selling her back to the people she wanted to get away from. I won't do that."

Mal shook his head. "How long do you think it will take her to get bored with life in Raglan? You've got an expedition booked right after the New Year. You're going to leave, and what is she going to do here all alone? Send her home to Hollywood. Collect your fee. She doesn't belong here, Ryan."

"I'm not going to do it. End of discussion."

Rogan took a step toward him. "Do you fancy yourself in love with her?"

"No," Ryan said. "I'm well aware we'd never make a go of it. Hell, she's a damn movie star. I can't offer her anything that she can't buy for herself." He paused. "Well, there are a few things that—"

"Let her go," Mal said. "You know you'll have to sooner or later. Just make a clean break now and send her back to her fiancé."

"I'm not going to listen to this," Ryan said. "She needs to make her own decisions. If she wants to go back, I'll take her. But I'm not going to try to convince her that marrying Ben Thayer is the right thing to do. He's cheated on her twice since they've been engaged."

"Really?" Dana said. "With who?"

"It doesn't matter," Ryan said.

"Someone is going to recognize her." Rogan warned.

"If they do, I'll take her down to the South Island and we'll stay there. She needs some time, and I intend to give it to her."

"Maybe you should send *her* the bill," Mal said.

"Right," Ryan said. "I'll do that." He tossed his coffee cup into the rubbish bin and started for the door.

"Don't go," Mal said. "Now that we're all here, I want to talk about the Everest trip."

"I already told you I wasn't going to do it," Ryan said.

"Just sit," Mal said, pointing to a chair on the opposite side of the table. "Give me ten minutes and then you can leave."

Reluctantly, Ryan pulled out the chair and straddled it. He rested his forearms across the back and waited, confident that nothing Mal could say would change his mind. "Amy's father has agreed to fund the entire expedition. Everything. He's bought us enough climbing permits to fund a full complement of support crew and Sherpas. But he's made it clear that his funding is contingent on all four siblings going along."

Ryan frowned. "Dana, too?"

"Yeah, Dana, too. She's going to work as the media liaison for Amy and *High Adventure* magazine."

Amy's father, Richard Engalls, was the publisher of *High Adventure* magazine and a climber himself. The multimillionaire saw a profit in their story and was willing to invest in the climb. But Ryan had a strong aversion to turning his family's tragedy into a money-making adventure.

"Engalls won't be satisfied with three out of the four Quinns?"

"No. But I do have a deal to offer you. This stays between the four of us."

"Oh, lovely. Another family secret," Ryan muttered.

Rogan shot him a dark look. "Tell him the plan, Mal."

"You come to base camp with us. You act as if you're going to do the climb, but at the last minute, you'll acquire an injury. A sprained ankle or a twisted knee. All you have to do is have a fall, and you can stay behind with the support staff. Engalls won't be able to pull the funding once we're on the mountain."

Ryan considered the plan. He wouldn't be forced to make the climb, forced to look at his father's body. He'd still be supporting a venture that he found a bit mercenary, but without his participation, his siblings wouldn't be able to go, and it meant a lot to them. "I'll think about it."

"I need your answer by the end of the week. If this trip falls through, we might as well close the doors and sell what we own."

Ryan groaned inwardly. After losing the Perry paycheck, he had to do something to make it up to his family. The Everest trip could draw enough publicity to finally put the business on solid footing. And then perhaps Ryan could finally strike out on his own. "All right, I'll go. There you have it. But I'm not going to make the climb."

Mal smiled. "Fine. Great." He turned to Rogan and gave him a high five. "Dana, you're going to Everest."

Dana's eyes sparkled with excitement. "I'm going to Everest."

"Roger Innis has a permit to climb, too," Rogan said. "He's going to want to get up there before us. What are we going to do if he arrives first?"

"We don't have to worry about that," Mal said.

"Why not?" Ryan asked.

Mal shrugged. "We just don't. Innis won't be able to find the spot."

Rogan sat down next to Mal. "What do you know?"

"Innis doesn't have the GPS coordinates. The party who found our father didn't feel it was right to publish that information until they'd talked to the family. They gave the coordinates to Mom and promised her that they wouldn't disclose them to anyone else."

"And you didn't think that was important to tell us?" Dana asked.

"Not until you all decided to go," Mal said. "Plus, Amy's father is going to leak the wrong coordinates. We won't have a problem with Roger."

Ryan pushed to his feet. "All right. I have to go. I'm counting on all of you to keep this thing with Serena quiet."

"Wait. One more thing. Since you're home, you can make it to the meeting with a new client at the end of the week. Ian Stephens is coming in to talk about an expedition he wants to fund."

"Who is Ian Stephens?" Ryan asked. "I've never heard of him."

"No idea," Mal replied. "He told Dana that he's the financial guy and that he wanted to meet with all of us. He'll be here on Friday morning."

Ryan nodded. "Okay, I'm in." Duffy followed him to the front door and walked out onto the porch with him. "Hey, I'm going to take Duffy home with me," he shouted.

"Sounds good," Dana replied. "Don't let him mooch. I've finally gotten him off human food. Don't mess it up."

"No human food?" Ryan said. "We're going to have to fix that. Come on, Duff, let's go."

He opened the passenger door of the Range Rover, and the dog hopped inside. "I've got a lady I want to introduce you to," Ryan said. "She loves dogs. You're going to like her. I like her a lot."

As he drove to the market, Ryan thought about his decision to go on the Everest expedition. Maybe it was time he finally faced his father's death full-on. With Serena here, Ryan sensed a subtle shift in his life, as if there were big changes just around the corner. And before he could turn that corner, he needed to leave his past behind.

SERENA STARED AT herself in the bathroom mirror. It wasn't horrible. It wasn't great, either. But it was a change, and at least she could say she didn't look like Serena Hightower anymore.

She picked up the box of hair color and held it up to her head, trying to match the color on the box with the color she'd gotten. "Ronaldo, I'm sorry."

Ronaldo Mercon had been her stylist for years. He'd been behind every major style change she'd made and had done her hair for all the awards shows. He'd made her look beautiful, and now she looked...ordinary.

She fought back a wave of emotion. It was like saying goodbye to her old life. She had no idea if she'd ever go back, but this change would help her go forward.

"Serena?"

"I'm in here," she called. "Wait out there."

"What?"

"Just wait and close your eyes."

She ruffled her damp hair and tried to make the uneven cut appear intentional. It wasn't perfect. But it wasn't that bad.

She found Ryan standing in the kitchen, his hand over his eyes. "Can I peek? Are you going to be naked?"

"No," she said.

"Should I get naked?"

"No. Just hang on." Her stomach fluttered and her self-confidence wavered. What if Ryan hated the new Serena? She'd never really considered what he'd think about her appearance. He'd fallen for a woman with long, honey-blond hair, and now her hair was a deep shade of mahogany with a blunt asymmetrical cut.

Fearing the worst, she raced back into the bathroom and slammed shut the door. It was awful. She hadn't been able to see the hair at the back of her head, so she'd just hacked it off. But even the bangs were crooked and the sides uneven. A professional could easily fix it, but how could she get her hair cut without risking recognition?

"Serena?" Ryan rapped softly on the door. "Are you coming out?"

"No," she called. "Not right now."

"What's wrong?"

"Nothing."

"You've shut yourself in the bathroom. Are you sick?"

"Kind of," she said.

"I'm coming in." He turned the knob and opened the door. She sat on the edge of the tub, her hands covering her eyes, waiting for him to say something.

"It's dreadful. I know it. But it's just temporary. I thought it would make me less recognizable."

She felt his touch on her hands and he slowly pulled her to her feet, then tipped up her chin. She waited, realizing that suddenly his opinion was the only one that counted.

"I like it," he said. "You look very exotic. And you're right, it *is* harder to recognize you."

"I did my best," she said.

He spotted her glasses on the edge of the sink, then put them on her face. Since her contacts were in, everything was blurred, but she gazed at her reflection in the mirror. "Better?"

"Now you look like a naughty librarian," Ryan said.

Serena took the glasses off. "The cut is kind of choppy."

"Isn't that how it's supposed to be?"

"Not really. And it's a bit darker than I intended."

"It suits you."

Overwhelmed with relief, Serena threw her arms

around his neck and gave him a fierce hug. "You're not going to say anything bad about it, are you?"

He pulled back and met her gaze. "No. Sweetheart, you could shave your head or color your hair bright blue, and you'd still be the most beautiful woman in the world."

She stepped over to the mirror again and grabbed the scissors. "Maybe you could just even out the back for me? I can't see it, but it feels a little ragged."

"I could try, but maybe we should call Dana. I know bugger all about cutting hair. And if I mess it up, you're going to cry."

"I promise I won't cry."

She watched in the mirror as he snipped away at the back. Then she showed him how to fix the sides. In the end, Ryan managed to make the cut much better. "I like it," Serena said.

"Now you're ready to meet another member of the family." He whistled softly and a few seconds later, a black Labrador came trotting into the bathroom and sat down at her feet.

"Who is this?" she said, patting the dog's head.

"That's Duff. Duffy. I thought you might enjoy having him around. If you want to take a walk on the beach or go into town, he can go with you."

Serena bent down and scratched the dog behind his ears. She hadn't seen her own dogs in over a month. "He's sweet."

"He's also a mooch. You can't leave any food out or he'll eat it. My sister brought pastries into the office for a meeting one morning, and he ate them all, along with half the cardboard box. He managed to open the refrigerator door once and pulled everything out. There was food everywhere."

"I have a dog—his name is Roscoe—and he pulls the flowers out of the garden. The gardener plants them and he yanks them out. The gardener plants them again and Roscoe yanks them out. I've had two gardeners quit because they can't stand my dog." She sighed. "I wish you could meet my dogs."

"Maybe I will someday," Ryan said. He walked back to the kitchen to unpack the groceries he'd bought, and Serena sat down on the stool at the other side of the island and watched him.

"What did you get for dinner?"

"Steaks," he said, holding up the plastic-wrapped packages. "Prawns. Some fish. I also got fresh vegetables and lettuce for salad." He pulled out a small carton and slid it across the counter. "And ice cream, to help you put on that fifteen pounds."

She held out her hand. "Spoon, please."

He reached into a drawer and retrieved a spoon for her. Serena opened the carton and scooped into it. The chocolate was rich and creamy, more like gelato than ice cream.

"I stopped at the office after I dropped you off."

"How did it go? Was Dana there?" She scooped out another spoonful and handed it to him.

"Everyone was. Mal, Rogan and Dana. I got a thorough tongue-lashing for sleeping with you. They think I broke up your engagement. I told them it was your decision."

"But you helped me make that decision. Without you, I'm not sure I would have had the courage to go through with it."

Ryan met her gaze and held it. "Yeah, I guess so."

An uneasy silence descended between them. "What is it?" she finally asked.

"I don't want you to regret anything," he said. "I don't want you to think that I pushed you into walking away from Ben. The only thing I ever wanted was for you to be happy."

"And I am," she said. "Look at me. I have ice cream, a new hairdo and a man who is fabulous in the sack. What more could a girl want?"

"A career?"

"I've invested my money well. And if I'm not making movies, I can sell my house in L.A. and my apartment in Manhattan. I'd be happy to live in a little cottage in the country with my dogs until I figure out what to do in the real world."

"Sounds like a perfect life," he said. He held up one of the steaks. "So, what will it be—steaks or prawns?"

"You know, since I changed my hair, we could go out tonight. We could have a pizza. I haven't eaten pizza in months."

"Is that what you want?" Ryan said.

"Yes," she said. "That is exactly what I want."

"Then get yourself dressed and—"

"I am dressed," she said, standing up and twirling around. "What's wrong with this?"

Ryan circled around the counter and pulled her body against his. He reached down and grabbed the hem of her skirt, slowly pulling it higher and higher on her thighs. "I don't know. What do you think might be wrong?"

She groaned and spun away from him. "All right, all right, I'll put on some underwear."

"You damn well better put on underwear. It's hard enough for me to concentrate when I'm around you. No use making it impossible."

Serena gave him a kiss, then headed for the bedroom. Was it possible to be any happier than she was right now? Yesterday could have been the worst day of her life, but instead, it had been the best, because Ryan had put her first. Though she knew there was trouble ahead, she felt as if she could handle anything, as long as Ryan was at her side.

RYAN STOOD ON the beach, staring out into the predawn sky. He looked down at his mobile and cursed softly. It had been forty-eight hours since they'd left Fiji, and neither he nor Serena had answered the calls accumulating on their mobile phones.

He scrolled through the numbers, then closed his eyes and pressed redial, waiting for the phone to connect. A few seconds later, he heard Perry's voice on the other end.

"Quinn! Where the hell are you? Never mind, I know where you are. The charter had to file a flight plan. You're in Auckland. Tell me that you have her with you?"

"No," he said. "She's not with me. But I know where

she is." Technically, it wasn't a lie. Serena was asleep, in his bed. "She's safe."

"Did you have anything to do with this?"

"No," Ryan said. "She told me that she'd called her fiancé, then asked me to come with her. I thought it best that I go."

"Perfect. Good man."

Ryan was misleading Perry, but he didn't care. His first priority was to protect Serena. His second was to try to salvage his business relationship with Perry for the sake of his professional reputation. "She's not going to get married," he said. "I'm pretty sure she's closed the door on that."

"Then, open it up again. You need to convince her to come back to L.A. and smooth things over with Ben. I've spoken with him and he's promised to keep this little dustup under wraps until he can talk to Serena. As far as everyone is aware, the wedding is still on. But we're not going to be able to keep up the facade if she doesn't return to L.A. at the end of the week."

"What about the bridesmaids?" Ryan asked.

"They've been paid very well. They won't talk to the media."

"You're going through an awful lot of trouble just to make sure your movie opening isn't spoiled," Ryan said.

"Millions. That's what this problem could cost us. Millions. No one is going to be talking about the movie."

"I thought any publicity was good publicity," Ryan said.

"That's something idiots tell themselves when they

pull some boneheaded move. I need a happy, glowing lead for my media tour. Get her back here."

"I'm not promising anything," Ryan said. "If she doesn't want to go, I won't force her."

"Then I'll send someone to fetch her myself."

"And I'll find a place for her to hide and she'll never come back." Ryan paused. "Just give her some time. Let her sort this out on her own. She's aware that she has responsibilities."

"And marrying Ben Thayer is one of them," Perry shouted.

"Sir, he cheated on her. Twice. I really don't think—"

"She hasn't been a perfect angel, either," Perry shouted. "Ask her about all of that." He took a moment to calm himself, and when he began again, his tone was more measured. "Why are you defending her? Don't dream that what you've had is more than it is. I know she can be very alluring. That's what makes her so great on the big screen. But you're just one in a long line of capricious adventures she's had with men. Believe me, she will grow bored with you and move on. And sooner than you think. I assume your sister told you the deal I offered?"

"She did," Ryan replied.

"If I were you, I'd take the money. Because you're not going to end up with the girl."

"I'll contact you after I talk to her." Ryan switched off the phone and cursed softly.

Why was everyone warning him off Serena? First Miles, then Perry. Even his family was unenthused. Could she really be as flawed as they said she was?

Sure, he'd met her only a few days ago, but Ryan had seen her at her worst and had found her sweet and kind, a woman without guile.

"But she's an actress," he murmured. Had he been fooled? Was she so skilled that she could pretend to be exactly the kind of woman he wanted her to be?

He'd always been clear on exactly what he wanted from the women in his life. And he was able to control his feelings, to stop himself from falling before he reached the point of vulnerability. But with Serena, that point had rushed by, somewhere above the South Pacific, right around the time she'd first kissed him.

Since then, he'd been infatuated to the point of blindness. But why would she try to fool him? What would that get her? Yes, he was protecting her, but he probably would have done the same even if she was a raving harpy. Though her motives weren't exactly clear, he couldn't imagine her engaging him for calculating reasons.

Unless she was the kind of woman who enjoyed the game. Was that all she wanted from him—entertainment? Ryan rubbed his eyes, then fixed his gaze on the rising sun.

This was what it was to fall in love, he mused. He'd have to trust her, without question. He'd have to expose himself to pain and betrayal. But if it was real, the reward would be worth the risk.

Ryan heard Duffy bark, and he twisted around to see Serena walking toward him, the dog at her side. She carried two mugs of coffee and handed one to him before sitting beside him in the sand. Duffy sat down in front of them both.

Serena chuckled. "He makes a better door than a window."

"Yeah, he is a talented dog." Ryan grabbed a nearby stick from the sand and tossed it toward the water's edge. "Go get it, Duff."

The dog took off and Serena leaned into Ryan. "Much better." She took a sip of her coffee. "What are you doing up so early? After last night, I assumed you'd want to sleep in."

"I'm just used to getting up before the sun," Ryan said. "We usually start climbing before dawn, so this *is* sleeping in for me."

"I guess my adventure hasn't been very exciting for you," she said.

"Oh, I wouldn't say that," Ryan replied. He stole a quick kiss, then glanced down at his phone. "I talked to Thom Perry this morning."

"What?"

He figured she'd be upset, but Ryan hadn't predicted the look of utter betrayal in her expression. He reached out, but she evaded his touch. "Let me explain."

"You don't have to. I understand. Your loyalty is to Thom, not me. You're just doing your job. So, how long did he give you to get me back to L.A?"

"He wants you there as soon as possible," Ryan said. "But I told him it was your decision. I also told him you weren't with me."

"How much is he paying you?"

"That doesn't make a—"

"How much?" Serena insisted.

"Double my fee if I get you back to L.A. Triple if you walk down the aisle. But, Serena, this isn't about me. As much as I'd like to keep you here, you've got some loose ends to tie up in L.A. You're going to have to go back. You have a contract that says you have to help promote your movie."

She stood up and brushed the sand off her pants. "It always comes down to money, doesn't it?" She laughed bitterly. "That's all I've ever been to anyone. A way to make more money."

Ryan scrambled to his feet and grabbed her hand. He pressed her palm to his bare chest, holding it there. "My only loyalty is to you, Serena. I will support you no matter what you decide to do. And I don't care about the money. From the moment I met you, it stopped being about a paycheck." She searched his eyes for the truth, and he leaned forward and touched his forehead to hers. "You have to believe me," he murmured. "I wouldn't lie to you."

Serena drew a ragged breath. "I—I need to take a walk."

"I'll come with you."

"No, I have a lot to think about. I'll be back later. You stay here and watch the sunrise. It's going to be beautiful."

Ryan watched her walk to the cottage and fought the urge to follow her. Maybe it was for the best. They'd been growing so close over the past few days, close enough for him to imagine some sort of future between them. They both needed a reality check.

His phone rang again, and he pulled it out of his shirt pocket and checked the screen. Ryan bit back a curse. It was a text from Ben Thayer: Please have Serena call me. Tell her I still love her.

They'd had two glorious days of freedom, and now the walls between them were coming back up again. Anger surged inside of him. Why had he allowed himself to be vulnerable now? And why Serena? He'd gone his whole life content that he'd spend it alone, afraid to give his heart to anyone who might destroy it. And now, by fluke, he'd found a woman he wanted, a woman he could imagine in his future. It wasn't supposed to be this difficult.

Hell, his two brothers had sailed through the process. In a matter of weeks, they'd found their perfect mates. Both had decided to make a home in New Zealand, giving up their lives elsewhere. But Serena was different. She belonged to her fans—and perhaps to Ben Thayer. She didn't belong to him.

7

SERENA JOGGED ALL the way from Ryan's *bach* to the business district of Raglan, Duffy trotting beside her the entire way. The town was a perfect mix of quaint shops and galleries, tantalizing cafés and pubs, and businesses geared toward the surf culture. Huge palm trees lined Bow Street, lending the town a relaxed, vacation vibe.

Though they were in the midst of summer in the southern hemisphere, the town was decorated for the upcoming holiday, Christmas lights hung from light poles and wrapped around palm trees. Maybe next year, she and Ryan could spend the holiday in London, where there was at least a chance of snow. But then, she might not even be with Ryan next week, let alone next year.

She found a spot to buy a latte, a bottle of water and the local newspaper, then walked to the end of the street and found a small park that overlooked the water. No one gave her a second glance or pointed and whispered. Her new hairstyle and sunglasses were enough to throw people off. And she'd managed a passable Kiwi accent.

She and Duffy found a comfortable bench and she gave him a drink from the water bottle before opening the paper. She scanned the articles and the advertisements, her gaze coming to rest on an ad for a local bakery.

"Help wanted," she murmured. Serena had always wondered what it would be like to live in the real world, to have a job that required her to work from nine to five. If she ever put her film career behind her, she'd want to do something else she enjoyed.

She'd always loved cooking and baking. Her youth had been spent sitting in the kitchen with her mother's housekeeper, watching her prepare meals and treats for the two of them. Good food had always meant home to her, even when her parents were away. But Serena's love of cakes and biscuits wasn't enough of a qualification to be hired in a bakery, and she'd want to work in the back so she wasn't recognized.

She read the requirements for the job, surprised that she did qualify. Jumping up from her spot, Serena tucked the newspaper under her arm and called to Duffy. She was curious. Would they even consider her a suitable candidate? This would be a good test. "Come on, boy. Let's go."

The bake shop was located right on Bow Street. Colorful patio tables were set out front, beneath striped awnings. She hooked Duffy's leash beneath the leg of a chair, dropped her things on a table and walked inside. She waited while two customers placed their orders, then stepped up to the counter.

To her surprise, Serena found that she was nervous.

It had been years since she'd had to compete for movie roles. Auditioning was a thing of the past. But here, in this little bake shop, she was no different from anyone else searching for a job. And that felt good.

"Hello," the clerk said. "What can I get you?"

"I read in the paper that you're looking for help," she said, responding in a Kiwi accent. "Is there an application?"

"Yes," the woman said. She walked over to the register and pulled a piece of paper out of the drawer beneath it. "Just fill this out," she said, handing the application to Serena. "Bring it back and we'll set up an interview with you. I'm the owner, Amanda. Are you from around these parts?"

"No," she said. "But I'm considering moving here."

"Great!" the woman said. "I moved here from the States about ten years ago. I married a Kiwi. It's a great place to live."

"Yes, I've noticed that."

"Everyone knows everyone else. There's a bit of gossip, but mostly people are very sweet. Have you worked at a bakery before?"

Serena shook her head. "No, but I've done a lot of home baking. And I had a wonderful teacher. And I learn fast."

The woman frowned. "Are you sure we haven't met?"

"No," Serena said, stepping back.

"You look familiar. Anyway, I'm hoping to open up a new shop in Hamilton, and I need to hire a few more people for this place. When would you be able to start?"

"Oh, I don't know. I'd prefer to bake than to handle customers. I'm not really sure I'd be right for the job."

Amanda laughed. "Well, why don't you leave that up to me. Fill out the application and we'll talk."

Serena nodded, checking on Duffy. "I really have to go. I have my dog outside, and I—"

"Is that Duffy?" the woman asked, peering through the wide glass windows.

"Yes. Yes it is. I'm just walking him for a friend."

"You're friends with Dana Quinn? She comes in here almost every morning. If you're friends with Dana, then I'm sure she'll give you an excellent reference. She hasn't been in this morning. I'll talk to her if she stops by."

"Please, don't bother her about this. I'll just look over the application and get back to you."

Amanda's hopeful expression fell. "Can I get you anything before you go? On the house. You should try our cinnamon rolls. They're so good you'll have to come work here."

"Sure. I'll take a cinnamon roll. And are those dog biscuits?"

"They are. Our own recipe."

"Give me five of those." Serena pulled some money out of her pocket, then gathered up her purchases, thanked the owner and walked out the front door. She sat down on one of the chairs and snatched up Duffy's leash. "Come here. I have a treat for you."

As she fed him the dog biscuits, Serena scanned the questions on the application. Most were simple enough to answer. Maybe running the shop would be fun, she mused. But then, she didn't know anything about making a business a success. She'd probably bankrupt the place in a matter of months.

She had to face facts: she was qualified to do just one thing in the world and that was act. And Serena was a good actress. She'd studied her craft and chosen the right films and she had a career that most actresses would kill for. She was on the verge of doing roles that would win her awards. She'd no longer be just a pretty face.

And putting down roots here didn't mean she had to give up her career. She'd done the math. L.A. was a thirteen-hour plane ride from Auckland. That was just a few hours longer than the trip from London to Los Angeles. Plenty of actors lived in Australia. Why not New Zealand?

Of course, she wouldn't be able to dash off to a meeting at a moment's notice or shop with her stylist. But she could have a career on her own terms.

Then again, putting a plan together might be a bit premature. She and Ryan hadn't really discussed the future. And after their argument this morning, it was quite clear that he expected her to go back to L.A. What if she refused? What if she just moved to Raglan and set up house?

Serena smiled to herself. Most men would be scared off by such an aggressive move. But telling Ryan about her plans would give her a clue to his feelings for her. Did he want her in his life, or was he just waiting for her to leave?

"Who stole my dog?"

Duffy leaped to his feet and trotted down the pavement to an approaching figure. Serena recognized Dana immediately and stood up. "Hello," she said.

"Hi," Dana replied, frowning. "Oh, my God. Serena! What have you done with your hair?"

Serena reached up to fuss with a curl at her temple. "I decided I needed a change."

"I barely recognize you. It's a big change. But it's really cute. Highlights your cheekbones. I see you've found my favorite bake shop."

"I have," Serena said, nodding.

Dana glanced down at the table. "You have a cinnamon roll. And a coffee. And—a job application?"

Serena winced inwardly. "Yes. I've been thinking about staying in Raglan for a while. I was just curious about the jobs available."

"Really?" Dana tried to appear unfazed by Serena's admission, but she was clearly having a hard time with it. "But why would you ever give up acting. You're so fabulous at it."

"Oh, I'm not saying I would."

"That's a relief. I like your films. But it would be great if you stayed in Raglan. It's not Malibu or L.A., but it's really nice here." She paused. "Do you really need to work in a bakery?"

"No. But I want to do something, and I was curious if I could even qualify for a regular job. Just reviewing my options."

Dana sat down at the table, and Serena had no choice but to join her. "Do your options include Ryan? Because he's a really good person. He's loyal and he's brave and he's smart and…and I've just made him sound like Duffy."

"I do care about him," Serena said. "I'm just not sure his feelings are mutual…yet."

"Give him time," Dana said. "It takes a lot for Ryan to trust. He took our father's death the hardest. He doesn't talk about his emotions easily. Or much else that's going through his head. But there's a really decent bloke in there." She paused to take a breath. "I can't believe I'm sitting here talking to Serena Hightower. It's so weird."

"If I stay in Raglan, we can talk every day," Serena said.

"If you really want a job, you could work for Max Adrenaline. Oh, it would be so nice to have another woman around the office. Sometimes those boys are just unbearable. I hoped maybe Amy or Claudia would want to help with the family business, but Amy's too busy with her writing and Claudia is still working in Sydney. We have loads of work to do before the Everest trip. Oh, and you have to meet my mum. She is a huge fan. I hope you don't mind, but I spilled the beans that you were staying with Ryan. She was shocked, I tell you, shocked. Ryan barely says a word about his personal life. We all wondered if he would ever—" Dana stopped short. "I should just stop talking. Full stop. So, what are you doing this morning?"

"I'm going to walk back to the *bach*. Maybe go surfing or do some reading."

"Let me drive you. My car is just down there," she said, pointing to a small blue Toyota.

."All right," Serena said. "But don't you have to get your pastries first?"

"Oh, where is my head this morning? I'll be right back."

"And don't tell Amanda who I am," Serena said as Dana rushed to the door. "She didn't recognize me and I'd rather just remain—"

"Incognito?" Dana asked. "I completely understand."

Serena watched Dana through the glass, wondering if the other woman would be able to keep her secret. There was no reason to make a spectacle of herself. And she loved the fact that she was able to walk down the street without anyone noticing. It had been years since that had happened, and it was wonderfully liberating.

Maybe she ought to change her name. She could go by the name on her passport—Ellsbeth Serena Sheridan. She hadn't been Ellsbeth since she was born. Her parents had always called her Serena. And she'd chosen to use her grandfather's name for her career. Hightower was a famous English acting family.

The thought of disappearing into a new place, without any of her old baggage was intriguing—and a bit exciting. But she'd have to make sure her secret stayed safe. No one could know she was in New Zealand.

Which meant it was time to make that call to Thom Perry. And to her former fiancé. They wanted her in L.A. in a matter of days and were both determined to take away the freedom she'd so recently realized she craved. And they had too many reasons to set the media on her trail.

RYAN SAT ON the front porch, his tent spread out on the plank floor. He found the tear that had come from an errant crampon and snipped a small patch from the repair kit he kept in his pack.

He'd been occupying himself with mindless tasks all morning, waiting for Serena to return. But it was nearly noon and she'd been gone since dawn—nearly six hours. If she wasn't back soon, he'd go looking for her. She couldn't have gone far on foot and with Duffy along. But then, maybe someone had recognized her and— He tossed the repair kit onto a nearby chair, then pulled his mobile from his pocket.

He stared down at the screen. He'd never gotten her number. Ryan cursed softly. His mind raced to all sorts of possibilities. She could be hurt. Or maybe she'd met some handsome surfer and was enjoying lunch with him now. Or maybe—

The sound of a car on the gravel drive interrupted his worry, and he jogged down the steps as Dana's Toyota pulled up to the *bach*. His sister got out, and a few seconds later, Serena followed. A sigh of relief slipped from his lips and he hurried over to help Serena with the sacks of groceries she was carrying.

"I'll get the things from the boot," Dana called.

"Thanks," Serena said.

"Hi." Ryan bent close and brushed a kiss across her cheek. "You've been busy." He grabbed the sack, and his gaze came to rest on her hair. It had changed again, the cut a bit shorter.

"I met Dana at the bake shop. She took me to her hairdresser to get my hair fixed and then we had a mani and a pedi and got to talking. And then I had to stop at the market because I wanted to cook a nice dinner tonight." She paused. "I'm sorry if I worried you."

He met her gaze and saw the regret in her eyes. "I'm sorry," he whispered. "It was my fault. I'm glad you're home."

Dana came around the rear of the car with another sack of groceries and a few bottles of wine. She set it on the porch, maneuvering around his tent. "All right. That should be it. Elly, I will see you later. Brother, be nice to her. I want her to stay around for a while. Oh, and I'm keeping Duffy. I know you've been feeding him human food."

Dana got back in her car and pulled out of the drive, waving as she passed Serena. Ryan waited until the car was out of sight before he turned to Serena. "Elly?"

"Ellsbeth," she said. "It's my real name. I was just trying it out."

"Ellsbeth is your real name?"

She nodded. "Ellsbeth Serena Sheridan. Hightower is my grandfather's name. No one calls me Ellsbeth, except my grandmother, and she died ten years ago."

"Why do you need to change your name?"

"If I start a new life, I'm going to need a new name. And if you call me Elly Sheridan, no one will ever know I was Serena Hightower. I can just slip into Raglan society as a whole new person."

"You're planning to stay in Raglan?"

"How would you feel about that?"

"I'm not sure," Ryan said. "Could you be happy here?"

"I think so," Serena said. "But only if you were happy to have me here."

Ryan walked toward the porch. This was crazy. He wasn't going to be responsible for her walking away from her career because she had some silly idea she could be happy in Raglan. It was obvious she was running away from her problems and she was using him as an excuse.

"You don't want me to stay," she said, following him into the cottage.

"No, that's not it." He set the sack on the counter and began to unpack it.

"What is it then?" Serena asked.

"I would love to have you here with me. For as long as you want to stay. But I think first you have to deal with the problems that you left in your old life. You assume that everything is ruined, that your career is over. But what if it isn't? What if you could have it all back? Would you want to stay then?"

"Yes," she said. "I don't want that life anymore. It's not real. This is real. Here with you is real."

"And did it feel that way when you were first with Ben?"

Serena cursed, then spun and walked away from him. Ryan knew at that moment that he'd hit a nerve.

"Why are we talking about Ben?" she asked, spinning around to face him. "Did you call him, too? Did he convince you that I belonged back in L.A.? I don't love him and I'm not going to marry him."

"He knows you're with me. He texted me right after

you left this morning." Ryan pulled out his mobile and found the message, then held it out to her.

She shook her head. "I don't want to read it."

"'Please have Serena call me,'" Ryan read. "'Tell her I still love her.'"

Serena clapped her hands to her ears. "I don't want to hear it." She grabbed a tomato from the counter and threw it at him. It hit the refrigerator, just missing his head.

Ryan circled the island and reached for her, but she evaded his grasp and walked to the sofa. But he wouldn't be deterred. He caught her and turned her around to face him.

"I can't offer you half of what you've made for yourself," he said. "I'm never sure where my next paycheck is coming from or even if it's going to come. I live in this crummy little cottage and drive a ten-year-old car. You live in a world of mansions and limousines and private jets and expensive diamond rings."

"You can offer me this," she said, grabbing his hand and placing it on her breast. "And this," she said, leaning in to kiss him.

Ryan groaned softly as she deepened the kiss, her tongue teasing at his lips until he reluctantly gave in. He yanked her against his body, forgetting the argument and focusing on the taste of her mouth and the feel of her body beneath his hands.

Serena reached for the hem of his T-shirt and pulled it up, smoothing her hands over his chest. It was as if they were playing their disagreement out as a seduction, each of them challenging the other with their desires.

He couldn't stop. He wanted her now more than he'd ever wanted her. And yet Ryan knew that this wouldn't solve anything. When it was over, they'd still face the same problems.

Serena reached for the tie on his board shorts and, when she'd undone it, pushed the shorts down to his knees. He was already hard, the need coursing through him like a raging storm.

Her clothes came off next in a frantic race to expose more skin. When they were both naked, Ryan picked her up and wrapped her legs around his hips, the tip of his shaft teasing at her entrance.

There was no time for foreplay and he didn't think to get a condom until after he was buried deep inside of her. His breath caught in his throat when he realized what he'd done, and Ryan tried to pull out. But she arched against him.

"No," Serena whispered. "It's all right."

"Serena, I—"

"It is," she said. "Trust me."

And there it was, Ryan thought. The one thing he couldn't seem to do. Why couldn't he believe she wanted him? Why couldn't he accept that she wanted to stay? He could believe in his own feelings, but he couldn't seem to accept hers.

Serena moved against him, and Ryan set her on the edge of the counter, sweeping the groceries away with his hand. She braced her hands behind her, her gaze fixed on his face as he slowly plunged deep and then pulled back.

It had started so quickly, but now he slowed it down,

each exquisite stroke driving her closer to her release. He felt the first spasm before he saw her reaction, and Ryan increased his pace until she dissolved in a series of breathless moans.

It took all his willpower to stop himself, to wait until she was nearly sated before he stepped over the edge himself. And when he did, the pleasure was deep and powerful, shattering his resolve and wiping away all the doubts he had.

He was in love with Serena Hightower. Or Elly Sheridan. Or whoever she wanted to be. It didn't matter. He had to keep her with him, no matter what the cost. And if there were consequences later, then he'd deal with them. For now he was happy, and that was enough.

"Tell me this is real," he murmured, his lips pressed against her neck. "That's all I need to know."

"It's real," she said, breathlessly. "It's very, very real."

Serena curled up against Ryan's body, her leg thrown over his hip, her head resting in the curve of his arm. "What is it about your kitchen?" she murmured. "It's like there's some kind of aphrodisiac hiding in the refrigerator. You open it up and bang, we're off to the races."

"We have a thing for airplanes, too," he said.

"We'd probably be great on the beach," Serena said. "And in a tent."

"Oh, I've never done it in a tent before. In fact, I've never slept in a tent."

Ryan chuckled. "We're going to have to change that.

You didn't get all the adventure you wanted on Fiji. Maybe we could take a few days and find an adventure here?"

"Yes," she said. "Let's do it."

Ryan sat up and raked his fingers through his hair. "We could leave now. I have to be back here at the end of the week for a meeting, so we don't have much time."

Serena jumped on top of him and kissed him. "There's nothing keeping us here. And if I get a real job, I'm probably not going to be able to take vacation days right away." Serena stretched out on top of him and pinned his hands on either side of his head. "But before we get up, I want to say something to you."

Ryan kissed her, then frowned. "You look so serious."

"I am," she said.

"If you want to do it again, I'm not sure I can," he teased. "Three times in one day is about my limit."

"No, I'm quite satisfied on that front. I just want you to know that I hear what you're saying. And I will consider it."

"Going back?" he asked.

Serena nodded. "I know I've left a big mess, but I just need to sort out how to handle it. And I will talk to Thom this week. I can't promise you that I'll talk to Ben, but I suppose I could write to him."

Ryan smoothed his hands through her hair. "That's a good idea. I want you to be sure that this is where you should be."

"I understand."

He gave her a fierce hug and rolled her over beneath

him. Serena brought her legs up along his hips, rubbing the back of his thigh with her foot. "So, Dana told me you're going to Everest. When do you leave?"

"Not for another two or three months. But I have a few trips before then. A two-week trek to Kilimanjaro and two ice-climbing classes in the Alps. Everest will be a long one. We'll be gone for almost two months." He stared down into her eyes. "This is what I do…for now. But it won't always be like this, I promise."

"How will it change?"

"Hopefully, after the Everest trip, business will increase and Mal will be able to hire more guides and I won't have to be away so much. I'll still take some groups but only the short trips."

"You probably don't want to hear this, but I have plenty of money. You don't have to worry."

"I'm not sure how long I'd be able to survive as a kept man. It might wear away at the ego a bit." He drew a deep breath. "I did have an idea for a new career path, though."

"Tell me," she said.

"There's a bloke here in Raglan who runs a surf school. He's getting ready to hang up his board, and I've been considering taking over and starting my own school. Or buying him out."

"You're a wonderful teacher."

"We could use the *bach* for a bunkhouse and find somewhere else to live."

"I'd miss the beach," she said. "And I like this place."

"I thought you might want something a bit more… posh," Ryan said.

"No, I'm happy with this," Serena said. In truth, she couldn't remember ever being happier than she was in his little *bach* on the beach. Maybe at her house in Kent, but that was only because of her dogs.

Her dogs. She'd have to charter a jet to bring them to New Zealand. Maybe the house *wasn't* big enough. The two of them and five dogs. One big, happy family.

She snuggled up against his chest. For the first time since they'd been together, Serena could see a way forward. It wouldn't be easy, but there was a chance they could make it work. And yet now that she knew Ryan's doubts, she realized that he wouldn't truly believe in her until she left her old life behind.

She thought about the reaction she'd get from the media when they announced the wedding was off. All the money spent on the ceremony and the guests who'd made a commitment to attend. People would want to know all the details of why she'd broken it off, and she had no doubt that Ryan's name would come up. He'd be painted as the villain and he didn't deserve that. This whole mess was her fault—for agreeing to the engagement, for letting it go on for so long and then for planning a wedding to a man she didn't want to marry.

"What's going through your head?" Ryan asked, pressing his lips against her temple.

"I'm just trying to think my way through this. It's going to be so messy. If I don't plan to ever go back, then maybe it is right to just walk away. The studio could sue me for breach of contract, but I doubt they'd want to do that. It would burn a bridge that they wouldn't want to burn."

He slowly stroked her hair as he listened, the simple caress soothing her nerves and calming her fears. "I could always just say I'm going into rehab. No one would question that. I've done it before."

"Have you?"

She nodded. "About five years ago. The partying got out of control and I was just exhausted. And the studio wouldn't insure me for my next movie unless I went. That reputation stayed with me for a long time. Everyone still believes I'm unstable."

"I don't," he said. He kissed her, his lips soft against hers, his tongue delving into the warmth of her mouth. Every problem seemed to disappear from her mind when his lips met hers. If only they could spend the rest of their lives kissing, she mused. Life would be perfect.

"I think we should leave for our camping trip tonight," Serena said. "Right now. Let's pack our bags and go."

Ryan rolled off her. "You've got ten minutes to pack," he said. "Take some warm clothes and sturdy shoes. If we need anything along the way, we'll buy it."

"Really? We can just leave?"

"Sure. We can do anything we want," Ryan said.

Serena closed her eyes. They could. Their lives belonged to them. No more managers or agents, no paparazzi or reporters, no more disappointed studio execs. For the next few days, they were completely free.

"Where are we going?" she asked.

"North," he said. "About five hours. We'll stop in Whangerei tonight. And then I'm going to show you one of my favorite places on the North Island."

Ryan packed his gear in a large backpack, leaving a smaller day pack for Serena. "I brought four suitcases to Fiji," she said. "I left with one. Now I'm going to be traveling with this." She glanced over the bed at him. "I'm so proud of myself."

"You haven't worn makeup since that last night in Fiji," he commented. "I like the way you look without it. And I like the hair." He grabbed her hand. "But these fingernails are not going to last."

She looked at her manicure and shrugged. "I did it for Dana. She was so excited to hang out for the morning. I think she's always wanted a sister. I have, too."

"Speaking of… Maybe you should call your parents and let them know where you are," he said. "Won't they be wondering?"

"I doubt it," Serena said. "I haven't seen my mom in five years and my dad in six or seven. We talk at Christmas and on my birthday, but that's all." She drew a deep breath. "So, now you've heard all my sad stories. Do you want to run away from me now or later?"

"Hmm, let me think," Ryan said. "I choose later. A lot later. Maybe never."

"All right," she said. "I gave you a chance. You're stuck with me." She zipped up the pack and tossed it his way. "And I am ready to go."

"That's what's great about you, Elly. You're a low maintenance kind of lady."

"Elly," she said. "I'm not sure if I'll be able to get used to you calling me that. I kind of like the way Serena sounds coming from you."

He rounded the bed and took her hand, pressing it to her lips. "Then, you'll be Serena to me."

She melted into his embrace, surrendering to a deep, passionate kiss. He'd seen into the darkest corners of her soul and still wanted her. But she couldn't get the comment he'd made out of her head. She'd believed she'd loved Ben, too, at first. Would this fade the way it had with Ben?

SERENA STARED OUT over the landscape and sighed softly. "It's beautiful." Ryan agreed, but he wasn't concentrating on the landscape. Instead, he was taking in all the perfect features of her face. She'd looked quite lovely, all painted up to go out to a club. But he liked her scrubbed clean, fresh-faced and completely herself.

She turned to Ryan and smiled. "How do you find these places? The waterfall in Fiji. This cove."

"This was one of my father's favorite spots. He used to bring us here to camp."

"You don't talk about him much," she said. "Why is that?"

"He died when I was eight. I remember him, but I'm not sure that all my memories are real. I think I may have embellished some of them over time. He was larger than life, tall and strong. And he had the bluest eyes. He used to dance around the kitchen with my mother. They'd put on the radio and just get lost in their own little world. We'd watch them, and I remember the way they looked at each other. They didn't have to talk." He chuckled softly. "They were mad for each other. Even a kid could see that."

"I don't remember a time when my parents loved each other. My first memories were of them fighting. Oh, and they *fought*. Crazy, plate-throwing fights. I can't imagine now what they were about. I was just six when they divorced. There was a huge custody battle that I read about later when I was in high school, but at the time, I was unaware of how bad it really was."

He slipped his arm around her shoulders and pulled her close. "I'm sorry."

Serena shrugged. "I think that's what led me to acting. I used to do a lot of pretending when I was younger. It was an easy escape. And I was always so much happier when I was pretending to be someone else."

"Where are they now?"

"My father lives in London with his mistress. He's on his fourth wife and he's cheating on her. My mother married an earl and lives in this huge country house. She has horses and raises prizewinning roses. And finds her husband terribly dull. So every couple of months, she jets off to Italy and stays with her boyfriend, Raoul, who is twenty years younger and fond of custom-made suits, which she buys him."

He took her hand and they hiked down to the beach. "You seem to be well-adjusted, considering all of that."

"Now I am," she said. "It took me years to straighten myself out. And I'm lucky I did. Things could have ended badly for me."

"What made the difference?"

"My first big film premiered in London, and they both came to see it and to celebrate with me. They got pissed and they each ended up crying on my shoulder. It turns out they're still in love with each other."

"Did you tell them?"

"God, no," Serena said. "My life is finally peaceful. If they're going to find each other again, they're going to have to do it on their own. But I realized how powerful love can be. It can raise you up to the highest heights or it can dash you on the rocks until you're in a million pieces."

When they got to the beach, Ryan slipped out of his backpack and unhitched his tent. He dumped the contents of the sack onto the hard-packed sand and began to sort through it. Serena squatted beside him, arranging the poles by length.

"I should thank you for saving me from a very big mistake," she said.

"Ben?"

Serena nodded. "I don't know what I was thinking. I guess I don't have any example to follow. I've never seen a happy marriage. I'm not sure what love looks like. I guess I believed the stability of marriage would be enough."

"When you explained it to me at the pool, I understood why you'd want that kind of arrangement, and you seemed to be going into it with your eyes wide open. But I'm glad you didn't go through with it in the end," Ryan said.

"Me, too." She drew a deep breath. "Are we going to put this tent together?"

Ryan showed her how to fit the pieces of the frame

into the pockets on the tent until they had a cozy little shelter.

"Look at that." She marveled. "It just popped right up. Can I go inside?"

"Sure," he said. "Unzip the flap on that side. And kick off your shoes. No sand in the tent. It's very abrasive on naked skin."

"We're going to get *naked* inside this tent?" she teased.

"I'm leaving the option open," he said.

Serena crawled inside and lay down on her back. Ryan did the same and they stared up at the ceiling. He'd never had a woman in his tent. "What do you think?"

"What happens if it rains?"

"It's waterproof."

"Or the wind blows?"

"I've slept in this tent in the middle of a monsoon."

"Is this the tent you'll take to Everest?"

Ryan shook his head. "I have six or seven tents. This is my general-purpose abode. My high-altitude tent is smaller and lower to the ground. It's more wind resistant."

A silence descended over the tent. He turned to look at her. "What is it? What has you worried?"

"If your father died on Everest, aren't you afraid that might happen to you?"

"I probably won't go up the mountain. I don't really want to remember my father that way. The plan is for me to help Dana at base camp."

She reached out and grabbed his hand, lacing his fingers through hers. It was such a simple gesture, but he always felt better when they were touching. Contact with her was like breathing. It made him feel alive.

Ryan rolled over on his side and slipped his hand around her waist. "I'm glad you're here," he said. "It doesn't seem to matter how much time we spend together. I always want more."

"Me, too," she said. "Sooner or later we're going to have to go our separate ways, though. We can't be attached at the hip 24/7."

"Why not? You look very nice on my hip."

"We lead very different lives, you and I. Under normal circumstances, we'd never have met."

"Probably not," Ryan agreed.

"Maybe it was fate. Or destiny. That's kind of a Hollywood story. I never really believed in it. But now I do," she said. "There's no other explanation."

"If I hadn't guided that Mont Blanc trip, I wouldn't have met Perry. And he wouldn't have hired me to go to Fiji with you, and we wouldn't be lying here right now."

"I guess we're lucky," Serena murmured. She pushed up on her elbow and leaned over him, brushing a soft, tantalizing kiss across his lips.

Ryan reached for her and furrowed his hands through the hair at her nape, pulling her into another kiss, this one deeper and more demanding. Their bodies fell against each other, fitting almost perfectly, as if fate had made them that way.

They'd grown to know each other well, to seek the spots that made each of them ache with desire, to move with the ebb and flow of seduction, first, one taking control and then ceding it to the other. They quickly undressed until they were both naked. Ryan pulled her beneath him, then slowly entered her, impatient to feel her warmth surround him.

There were times when they took things slowly and other times when their encounter was quick and desperate. This one would be slow, tender. As he moved above her, he took in the tiny details of her face, committing them to memory, etching them in his mind.

He'd had many women in his life, some that he'd never thought about again. That wouldn't be the case with Serena. No matter what happened between them, she would always be the woman he could never forget.

That might be a curse, but Ryan wanted to believe it was a blessing. They could have a future together. As he brought her to her peak, he could taste the words on his lips. He fought the impulse to say them. He was sure they were true, but until she dealt with her other life, they'd never be real. He would wait for a sign and then Ryan would tell her exactly what was in his heart.

8

THEY SPENT THE next two days in Northland, a wind-swept spit of land in the northernmost part of New Zealand. They hiked along deserted beaches and camped in secluded coves. It was a chance to learn more about each other and to discover what Ryan had always known—they were perfectly compatible.

He realized that this was what had drawn Mal to Amy, and Rogan to Claudia. This easy, effortless companionship. He couldn't imagine wanting to be with anyone else. And yet he knew that the clock was ticking. Though she hadn't said it, he suspected she was talking herself into returning to L.A.

Part of him hoped that she would just throw it all away. By burning every last bridge, she'd have no choice but to stay with him. And he didn't want to risk losing her. The idea of living his life without her caused a deep and undeniable ache. Like a hole in his soul. He suddenly understood what his mother had gone through, losing the man she'd loved in such a tragic way. And he also understood why she remained alone. Sometimes there was just one perfect match. For Ryan, it was Serena.

And yet his rational side kept reminding him that he'd have to let her go eventually. But not now. They still had a few days to enjoy the fantasy.

"Are you sad to be going back?" she asked.

They sat in a small café in Russell, a village that overlooked the Bay of Islands. They'd packed up their campsite at dawn and driven into town for brekkie. Soon they'd take the ferry across the bay to the highway and south to Raglan. They had a five-hour drive home in front of them, but Ryan had decided they'd take their time and stop along the way.

"I am," he said. "I wish I didn't have a meeting, but Mal says it's important. Some big client from England. He wanted us all there."

"My bridesmaids would have left Fiji by now."

"Fiji seems like another lifetime," he said.

"L.A. seems like lifetimes ago," she countered. "I don't even know how I lasted that long."

"There must have been something good about it," Ryan said.

"I enjoyed the work," she said. "I loved becoming someone else. And those moments when I'd lose myself in my character. All my problems would just disappear and I'd get to live someone else's life for a few minutes. It was everything that came with being a celebrity that was so hard to take."

Ryan grabbed his coffee and took a sip. He'd tried to bury his doubts deep over the past few days. But now that they were heading home, they'd bubbled to the surface again.

She was a good actress, that much he knew. And she could play a part with amazing ease. Was that what she was doing now? Had she convinced herself that this character, Elly Sheridan, was the person she wanted to be? And how long would she be willing to continue the charade, if it was a charade?

Ryan wanted to believe they were meant to be together, but he still couldn't put aside his last bit of doubt. It was as if he were on a roller coaster, up and down, certainty and doubt, back and forth until he wasn't sure what he felt.

"I think I'm going to have to watch your movies," he said.

"I can't believe you haven't seen one. I'm a bit insulted."

"I don't have a television," he said.

"You can watch movies on your computer. On your phone."

"I'm usually in spots without internet service."

"That's no excuse."

"All right," he said. "If I have to watch one movie, which one should I watch?"

"Oh, that's a hard question," she said. "If you—"

"Are you Serena Hightower?"

Ryan glanced up to see a teenage girl standing next to their table. He held his breath, wondering what Serena would say and how she'd react. Serena closed her eyes and drew a deep breath. "I was," she finally said.

"Mom!" The girl motioned to her family. "I told you it was her."

The family of four approached the table, and Serena pasted a smile on her face. She pulled her hand from beneath Ryan's and stood. He cursed inwardly, silently observing the scene unfolding in front of him.

"You look so different," the girl said. "I barely recognized you. What are you doing here?"

"Just taking a short holiday," Serena said.

"So are we!" the girl said. "We're from Seattle. I'm Becky and this is my mom, Ruth, and my dad, Harold. And my little sister, Katherine. Can we get a picture? My friends won't believe I met you. They don't even know where New Zealand is."

"Sure," Serena said.

They moved over to a barrel filled with flowers, and Serena dutifully stood in the center of the group and smiled as a waitress took the photo. After that it was a free-for-all as other patrons begged for a photo or an autograph.

Twenty minutes later, Serena returned to the table. "Let's get out of here," she murmured, "before someone else comes along." She glanced down at her uneaten meal and grabbed the scone she'd ordered.

"I paid the bill," Ryan said. He walked with her to the Range Rover and helped her inside, then got behind the wheel. "Are you all right?"

Serena nodded. "I guess I assumed I wouldn't run into fans in the middle of nowhere." She turned to him. "Those photos will probably already be all over social media. The entertainment shows will pick them up by the end of the day, and they'll spin the story in every direction. What am I doing in New Zealand? Who was the man I was with? What's happening with my wedding? Ryan, I think I just ran out of time."

Ryan noticed a woman approaching the car with a camera. He quickly started the engine and pulled away from the restaurant. When he glanced over at Serena, he saw tears swimming in her eyes. He felt a sharp ache in his chest as regret welled up inside of him.

"Hey, don't cry. We're fine."

"No," she said. "We're not. I'm not."

He drove toward the ferry landing, then parked the car along the side of the road. Reaching over, he pulled her into his arms, pressing a kiss to the top of her head. She cried for a long time, curling up in the seat when he had to drive the Range Rover onto the ferry.

When her tears had finally stopped, he helped her out of the car and they walked to the bow of the boat, where they stood at the rail as the ferry skimmed over the bay. Her dark hair blew in the breeze, and Ryan reached out and dried an errant tear from her cheek.

"Yesterday I was remembering one of my favorite movies. It's called *Roman Holiday*. Audrey Hepburn and Gregory Peck."

Ryan shrugged. "It's a good movie?"

"One of the best. In fact, Thom is thinking of doing a remake and they've been talking to my agent. I even have the haircut for it now."

"Do you want to do the movie?" he asked.

"No. I mean, sure, it would be a great role, but I would never want to try to top Audrey." She paused, staring out at the water. "It's a story about a princess who escapes the bonds of her position for a day. She meets a reporter, only she doesn't know he's a reporter, and they have this wonderful adventure in Rome. He thinks he's going to write a story about her, but instead, he falls in love. She falls in love with him, too, and it's so romantic and wonderful."

"And she runs off with him?"

"No," Serena said. "She gives him up. She realizes that she can't stop being who she was born to be. They were from two different worlds."

"That's not us," he said.

"Isn't it?"

He pulled her into his arms and held her close. But as they stood on the deck, Ryan found himself watching the people around them, wondering if they recognized her. He wanted to protect her from them all, to shout at the world for privacy.

But this was her world, this place where everyone recognized her and everyone wanted a little piece of her. He didn't want to share, and yet he knew that she couldn't just fade into obscurity.

Like the princess in the movies, she'd been born into this life. Her talent and her beauty had destined her for this all along. And he'd been a fool to hope the world would let her go without a fight.

SERENA OPENED THE screen door and called for Ryan. But the cottage was empty. She walked through to the back door and out onto the deck, then down the narrow path to the beach. She found him there, sitting on the sand, his wet suit pulled down to his waist and his surfboard lying next to him.

The wind was high and the waves rushed against the shore. She stood over him, then gave him a gentle bump with her knees. He looked up and grinned. "You should have come down earlier," he said. "Before the wind picked up, the waves were perfect for you."

"I'm not sure I can deal with the cold water," Serena said, sitting down beside him.

"You'll get used to it. You won't be able to stay away. That's the thing about surfing. Once the bug catches you, it won't let go." He ran his fingers through his wet hair. "Where have you been?"

"I drove into town. I had a few errands." She reached into her jacket pocket and pulled out an envelope and handed it to him.

He opened it and sighed. "Auckland to Los Angeles. Tomorrow. 7:15 p.m."

Serena nodded. "I need to go back before the wedding. It's just after Christmas. And I'm the one who is going to have to deal with it. I called Thom and told him to expect me."

"Then you're going to marry Ben," Ryan said, the words thick in his throat.

"Oh, God, no!" she cried. Serena laughed. "I'm sorry, I didn't phrase that well. I'm going to L.A. to call it off as soon as possible. Guests have to cancel their travel plans. My parents are flying in. I'm not sure I can stop that from happening. And Ben and I are going to have to come up with a plausible story to sell to the media. Thom promised that the studio would help with damage control." She wrapped her arm around Ryan's shoulders and kissed his cheek. "But I'm coming back." She pulled out another envelope and he took it from her fingers.

"What is this?" He withdrew the second ticket. "For me?"

Serena nodded, resting her chin on his shoulder. "I know you have to leave to go on your expedition in January. But I was hoping you could come and stay with me while I'm doing the West Coast publicity. And maybe you could come to New York, too? We could have another adventure. It will go so much easier if you were with me. And we could spend the holiday together." She paused. "I don't want to go back without you."

Serena realized it was a long shot. He had responsibilities here. And he'd probably want to spend Christmas with his family. But she couldn't bear being so far away from him for that much time. "Please?"

"Sure," Ryan said. "I think I can take some time away. As long as I'm back by the fifth of January, I'll be able to prep for Kilimanjaro. In fact, I could probably fly out from New York and have Mal take care of the prep here."

"We could spend New Year's Eve in New York," she said.

"Do you always do publicity after the film is released?"

"Thom made an accommodation for me, because of the wedding. I did a lot before I left for Fiji. We started in mid-November. But I have to finish it now. Plus, they want to push the junket into January because of awards season."

"Does the timing of the junket affect the awards?"

Serena giggled. "You really don't know anything about movies, do you? The film won't be eligible until next year. And I don't think it will get any nominations. It's a fluffy romantic comedy."

"Well, I know about you," he said. Ryan pulled her into his lap and kissed her. "Isn't that more important than all that other rubbish?"

"It is rubbish, isn't it?"

"I supposed you're going to have to help me pack. I have no idea what people wear in Los Angeles. I don't own a suit."

"You won't need a suit. Do you have a sports coat?"

"No, but I'm sure Rogan does. He's much better with fashion than I am. Plus he spends a lot of time in Sydney now, so he has city clothes. Should I bring a tie?"

"Probably not. If it's necessary, we'll just buy you one."

Ryan stood up and held out his hand to her, pulling her to her feet. Reaching back, he dusted the sand off her skirt. "What time is your meeting?" Serena asked.

"At three this afternoon," he said. "But if I'm leaving for a week or two, I'm going to have to go in and lay the Kilimanjaro expedition out for Mal and Dana."

"Do you think they'll object to you being gone?"

"No," Ryan said, shaking his head.

Serena breathed a sigh of relief. In truth, she was surprised that he'd agreed to come. But then, Ryan was accustomed to surviving in rough conditions. If he could climb Everest, then he could certainly handle a week in L.A. and another in New York. Maybe she could get him to London on his way back from Kilimanjaro—wherever that was.

"I bought us an early Christmas present today," she said. "A new bed."

Ryan blinked in surprise. "You bought a bed?"

"Actually, a whole bedroom. A double bed is kind of small for the two of us, especially when my dogs come. I definitely want more drawers, and your furniture is a bit of a—" She stopped. "Are you all right?"

"Of course," Ryan said. "I'm just—" He cleared his throat. "If we needed a bed, you should have told me. I could have bought it."

"But I wanted it to be a gift. I just assumed you'd be all right with it. Your mattress is so lumpy, it's as if I'm sleeping on rocks."

"You bought a mattress, too?"

"Yes… Are you angry with me?"

"No," Ryan said, staring out at the horizon.

She sat next to him, wondering what was going through his head. There were moments when he seemed so far away, and others when she didn't believe they could get any closer. Had she been wrong to invite him to the United States with her? Was it too soon to ask so much of him? And what was his problem with new furniture for his bedroom?

Serena tried to imagine what it might be like for him, stepping into her world. She recalled what it had been like in Fiji. His impressions about the plane and the house, the limitless bank card. Though her house in

Malibu wasn't grand, it was certainly more posh than Ryan's cottage. And on tour, there would be limos and restaurants and money being tossed about as if it were confetti at a parade. It was that sort of thing—and Ryan's reaction to it—that Serena worried about.

"I think I'm going to go out and surf a few more sets," he said. He pulled his wet suit up over his arms, then reached around for the zipper.

Serena stood behind him and pulled it up, then ran her hands over his shoulders. "I'll make some lunch. And I'll call Thom and tell him when we'll arrive. You're sure about coming along?"

He turned and slipped his arms around her waist. "Yes. I'm sure. But go through my clothes and pick out what you think I'll need. I don't want to look like some wally from up the boohai."

"I have no idea what that means," she said.

"It means I don't want to embarrass you."

"You'd never embarrass me. You're a handsome, clever, fascinating man."

"Who knows bugger all about the movies." He frowned. "What was the name of that movie you were telling me about? The one with the princess?"

"Roman Holiday."

He repeated the name softly. "All right. Well, I'll be up in a bit." Ryan brushed a quick kiss across her lips and handed her the tickets. Then he picked up his surfboard and ran out into the water. Serena watched him for a long time, her hand shading her eyes from the midday sun.

He was beautiful, the way he skimmed across the

waves, his arms thrown out. He'd bend and twist until he got the last bit of speed from the wave and then he'd turn sharply and drop down onto the board, paddling out for another set.

It was as if he'd been born to live in the midst of all this natural beauty. The sun, the sky, the sea. She made a mental note to plan a day of surfing for him in Malibu. It was winter in the northern hemisphere. He'd need to bring his wet suit and a board. But at least he'd be able to do something he loved on his visit. And she'd take him to see the redwoods. Though she'd never been, Serena had heard they were lovely.

She walked back to the cottage and wandered inside, running her fingers along the edges of the ticket envelopes. She found her mobile on the counter and picked it up, searching through the directory for Thom's office number. When she found it, she dialed the number and waited for his assistant to answer.

"Hello, Denise, it's Serena Hightower. Could you let Mr. Perry know that I'll be in Los Angeles tomorrow at 11:30 a.m.? Air New Zealand. Please send a car and open my house in Malibu. I'll also want to meet with Miles to discuss the rest of the publicity tour. If he has any questions, we can discuss them then."

They went over a few more details before Serena rang off. Then she sat down on one of the stools and cupped her chin in her hand. Once again, she felt her life shifting beneath her feet. She'd felt the same that night on the plane to Fiji. And again, on the jet to Auckland. And now she'd be flying back to where she'd begun.

So much had happened, she didn't feel like the same

person. And maybe she wasn't. She felt more like Elly Sheridan than Serena Hightower. And now she'd have to transform herself back again. The prospect made her utterly exhausted. It was a part she almost couldn't bear to play.

It had taken her years to discover who she really was. And she'd found herself the moment Ryan had stepped into her life. It had happened so quickly that she was afraid to believe it was real. But then she'd try to imagine life without him, and everything seemed to fall apart.

This was what love was—this crazy, frightening, exhilarating carnival ride. And she was afraid if she got off now, she'd never be able to hop on again.

L.A. would be the test. If they could survive that, they could survive anything.

"WHAT ARE YOU doing with my laptop, Ryan?"

Ryan glanced up to find Dana standing over him, her hands hitched on her waist. "I'm watching something."

"What?"

"A film. It's called *Roman Holiday*."

Dana pulled up a chair. "Oh, I love that film. Audrey Hepburn. And Gregory Peck. He is so handsome in that. Did you get to the part where he puts his hand in the gargoyle's mouth? Oh, and the end is so sad. You just know she wants to stay with him."

"It's already over." Ryan closed the laptop and handed it to her.

"What did you think? Did you like it?"

"I liked the motor scooter. The Vespa. Seemed fun."

"That's all you got out of it? The Vespa?"

In truth, Ryan had got a lot more out of the movie than that. But he didn't want to discuss any of it with his sister. He wasn't going to tell her how the movie mirrored his relationship with Serena or how he felt as if the two of them were as doomed as Joe and Princess Ann. Hell, Serena even resembled Audrey Hepburn with her flawless features and new haircut.

"I came to get you. Mr. Stephens will be here in five minutes."

"Fine," Ryan said. He followed Dana out of the office, but as he was walking through the reception area, he saw his mother walking in. Ryan stopped short. "Mum? What are you doing here?"

"Hello, darling," she said, crossing to his side.

Ryan kissed her cheek as she gave him a warm hug. "I understand you have a new girlfriend. A movie star. I'm not pleased that I had to hear the news secondhand from your sister. But I won't hold it against you if we all have dinner together tonight."

"Mum, I'm not sure I want to introduce Serena to the entire family at once. She met Dana. That's enough for a while."

"Why? We're a nice lot. Is there something wrong with her?"

"No!" Ryan said. "She's perfectly fine. All right, after our meeting, I'll ring her up and see if she'd like to join us for dinner. But why are you here now?"

"For the meeting," she said.

"They're still waiting for this Ian bloke to arrive. Let me make you a cup of tea." They walked into the kitchen, and he found a clean mug, switched the pot on to boil. She sat down at the table and pointed to the spot across from her.

"You might as well come out with it," she said. "I can tell you want to talk about her."

Ryan pulled out the chair. "How do you know if you're in love, Mum? Is there some kind of sign? Because I'm pretty sure that I love her, but this is all new to me. I'm sure I have it all sorted out and then she'll say or do something and I'll realize that I haven't got a clue."

"No one really knows until they know," Lydie said. "And sometimes they're wrong."

"That's very helpful, Mum. Could you be any more obtuse?"

"Don't insult me, Ryan. I'm your mother."

"Sorry."

"All I can say is that you'll know. Trust me on this. Your brothers knew. I knew. Something will happen, and it will all become clear and you'll realize that you can't live without this person." Her voice caught and she smiled. "And sometimes, you don't have a choice in the matter."

"Why didn't you ever marry again, Mum? I know there were men who were interested."

"I never met another man who caught my fancy. I had children to raise, a job to do. There just wasn't time for another person in my life."

"But it would have made things so much easier for you."

"Would it? It would have taken a very special person to raise another man's children. To love them and support them. And I didn't want a man to come between us."

"But we're not living at home anymore. Why not now? You could date."

"Who says I'm not?" Lydie asked. She stood up. "Come along, sounds like Mr. Stephens has arrived, and they're probably waiting for us." She made a quick cup of tea, then followed Ryan out of the kitchen.

They walked into the conference room together. Like Ryan, his siblings were surprised to see their mother there, and when she said hello to Ian Stephens as if they were old friends, the confusion grew.

"Sit down, everyone," Ian said. "I'm sure you're wondering what this is all about. Your mother suggested I use the ruse of being a potential client so that I could bring you together to discuss something that affects all of you."

"What is this about?" Mal asked. "Mum, is everything all right?"

"I contacted your mother first so that I could confirm some details, which she was kind enough to do. You are all the children of Maxwell Quinn, born 1958 in Queensland, Australia. Your grandfather was Conal Quinn, born in Ireland. Your grandfather was the elder brother of my employer, Miss Aileen Quinn."

Dana gasped. "*The* Aileen Quinn? The author?"

"Yes," Ian said. "Miss Quinn was sent to an orphanage when she was very young and her four brothers were scattered to the winds. When she learned of their existence, she set me on the task of finding all of their heirs so that she might leave them each a portion of her estate. You have many cousins who have already been beneficiaries of Miss Quinn's generosity, and now you will number among them."

Mal held up his hand. "Wait a second. You're here to give us money?"

"Yes," Ian said. "As the children of Max Quinn you are each entitled to a share of what Miss Quinn is giving away. There are a few requirements, however. You must submit to a DNA test to prove your connection to the family. And you must agree to visit Miss Quinn at your earliest convenience so that she might meet you. She's ninety-eight years old, so I would suggest you book a ticket sooner rather than later."

"How much money are we talking about?" Rogan asked.

Ian Stephens opened a file folder and glanced down at a piece of paper. "Five hundred and eighty-six thousand dollars," he said. He glanced up and looked around the table. "Each. There is an equal amount that you'll receive after you've met Miss Quinn. It is her hope that you'll use the money to follow your dreams."

"Jaysus," Mal said. "Is this some kind of joke? Are there hidden cameras?"

"I can assure you, Mr. Quinn, this is no joke. As soon as your relationship is confirmed by the DNA test, you'll all be quite well-off."

The silence in the room was deafening. Ryan was gobsmacked, unable to put a sentence together. Could this be true? If it was, then he finally had the means to step away from the family business and start his surf school. Mal had the resources to hire new guides. And

Rogan would have the chance to travel the world, taking photographs.

"What about Mum?" Ryan asked.

"Since she is not a direct heir to Conal Quinn, she will not receive a share. But there is nothing to stop you from giving some of your money to her."

"You knew about this?" Rogan asked, turning to their mother.

Lydie Quinn nodded. "I did. Mr. Stephens contacted me several months ago, but we needed to get all the paperwork in order and make certain that we were the right Quinns. And we are."

"Aileen Quinn," Dana sighed. "First, I meet Serena Hightower and now I'm going to meet Aileen Quinn. You can tell her that I'll be there next week. I'm quite anxious to meet her."

Ian smiled. "I'm sure she'll be happy to hear that. Now, if there's nothing else, I will leave you to discuss your great fortune."

"Mr. Stephens, there is one thing I would like to discuss before you leave," Lydie said. "There is another heir that you should contact. My husband had another child. Another son."

The room went silent, and Ryan and Rogan exchanged looks. "You know about him, Mum?" Ryan asked.

Lydie stared at Ryan. "*You* know about him?"

"I do. So does Rogan. How did you find out?"

Mal cleared his throat. "What are we talking about here? How can we have another brother? Mum, where have you been hiding him?"

"He's not mine," Lydie said. "His mother is Annalise Montgomery. She's an American and the boy is about twenty-seven, perhaps twenty-eight. About the same age as the twins. Now, how did you two find out about him?"

"I overheard someone gossiping about it on an expedition," Rogan explained. "And Ryan and I met him once. Dad took us to the office in Rotorua and she showed up with him. We were about five or six."

"Why didn't you say anything to me?" Mal asked.

"Because it wasn't your secret to keep," Ryan replied.

"Well, there it is," Lydie said. "Mr. Stephens, I'm sure you'll do the right thing. I can't give you much more information."

"She's quite a well-regarded climber," Ryan said. "I'm sure if you do an internet search you'll find her. I believe she lives near Seattle?"

His mother eyed him, then nodded. "Yes. Well, it's not a secret anymore."

"Why couldn't I have a sister?" Dana asked. "Why another brother? I don't want another brother."

Ian Stephens said his goodbyes and left the family to ponder the turn that their lives had suddenly taken. Mal was obviously curious about his new half brother. "How did you find out, Mum?"

"Your father took out a life insurance policy listing Annalise Montgomery as the beneficiary. After he died, the insurance company called me to ask if I knew who she was."

"He left money for her and nothing for you?" Mal asked.

"Your father believed that I would be covered through the company's life insurance. He wasn't aware that Roger hadn't paid the premiums in a year and a half. So we might have been left with nothing, but no matter. We all survived just fine."

"You deserve a share of Aileen's inheritance," Dana said. "We'll pool our money and divide it by five." She looked around the table. "Agreed?"

They all nodded. Lydie Quinn smiled. "I'm sure we'll discuss this all later. If we're finished here, I'd like to go and meet this movie star that Ryan has been dating."

"She's living with him," Dana said.

"And that's the reason we never tell Dana a secret," Rogan teased.

"And she prefers to be called Elly now. Elly Sheridan. That's her real name," Dana said.

Ryan stood up and walked over to his mother. "All right. But I want you to behave yourself. There has been no marriage proposal, she is not about to become your daughter-in-law, and I would appreciate if you keep stories about my dating history to yourself."

"Is that all?" Lydie asked.

"No," Ryan said. He turned back to his siblings. "I'm going with her to L.A. tomorrow evening. Mal, I'll need you to cover the prep on my Kilimanjaro trip. I hope I don't have to remind you how many preps I've done for you in the past year."

His brother nodded and Ryan walked out with his mother. "You were quite firm with them," Lydie said.

"I figured I'd hit them while they were still reeling

from their windfall." He chuckled softly. "I can't believe that just happened. It's like winning the lottery."

"I'm happy for you," Lydie said. "I know you haven't been entirely satisfied working for your brother. But now you have your own money to do with as you please."

Ryan grabbed his mother's hands. "Mum, I think you should hold off on meeting Serena for a bit. It's not that I don't want you to meet her, but we're not quite at that point yet."

"Are you in love, darling?"

Ryan didn't even have to think before he answered her question. "Yes. I am."

"Then don't screw this up," she warned. "I want all my sons married. I need grandchildren."

"What about Dana?"

"She's still young."

Ryan bent and kissed her on the cheek. "Go buy yourself something new, Mum. You're about to be a wealthy lady."

He walked out of the office and hopped in the Range Rover. As he drove out of town, he couldn't help but smile. Strange how life could turn on a dime. What would happen next?

He thought about his plans for a surf school and what he could do with a million dollars. He could make a life for himself and for Serena. He'd have something to offer her. But for now he'd keep his good fortune to himself. Until a check was in his hand, he couldn't trust that it was true.

9

"LADIES AND GENTLEMEN, we're beginning our final descent into Los Angeles International. Local time is 11:27 a.m. Please fasten your seat belts and return your seat backs and tray tables to their upright positions. Stow all carry-on in the overhead bins or beneath the seats. And thank you for flying Air New Zealand."

Serena gave Ryan's hand a squeeze and he smiled. He'd been reassuring her for most of the trip across the Pacific, but the closer they got to Los Angeles, the more anxious and frantic Serena became. He'd never witnessed such a change in character, and he was at a loss to explain how a woman so strong and confident could fall apart in such quick order.

"Everything is going to be fine," she murmured. She had said the words over and over again, but Ryan knew she wasn't convinced. He also knew she was more worried about him than about her own problems.

Ryan was surprised at how easily he could read her thoughts now that she was under stress. Serena was concerned that he would see or hear something that might alter his feelings for her.

He stared down at their linked hands. He loved her. Nothing would change that. But it was clear that his presence in Los Angeles was not going to help. If anything, he was adding to her distress. Gone was the bright, smiling beauty he'd spent the last week with, and in her place, a neurotic, whinging stranger.

The plane gently dropped out of the sky and she gave his hand another squeeze as the wheels touched down. Ryan looked out the window. He'd traveled through Los Angeles in the past, on his way to one exotic location or another. But he'd never thought it wise to stay and visit. He had to question his decision now.

Ryan helped Serena gather her things and they walked down the Jetway ramp, collected their luggage and headed toward Customs and Immigration. On top of everything else, Serena was jumpy and irritable after so many hours without sleep. She snapped at him when he offered to carry her bag, and when he suggested that he fetch them both a coffee, she shook her head, her lips pressed tightly together.

They headed out into the terminal and barely took ten steps before Ryan saw Thom Perry and Miles Du-Mont waiting for them. "Here we go," he muttered.

Serena noticed them at the same moment and reached for him, her fingers clutching his forearm. "You can do this," he said.

"We should have never come back."

"Serena, darling," Thom said, approaching with his arms held wide. "It's so good to have you here."

"Thom," she said as he kissed both her cheeks. "What are you doing here? Airport transportation usually isn't your responsibility."

"I thought we could talk on the ride," he said. He turned to Ryan. "Quinn. Great to see you again. And job well done. I knew I could count on you."

Serena glanced over at Ryan, frowning. "What is he talking about?"

Ryan grasped her arms and moved her away from the two men. "Will you excuse us for just a moment," he said.

"Miles, why don't you take the luggage to the car and wait for us there," Thom ordered. He reached in his suit jacket pocket and withdrew an envelope, then held it out to Ryan. "I expect that will cover it."

"I don't want your money," Ryan said.

"But we had a deal."

"What deal?" Serena said, her voice trembling.

"Excuse us," Ryan said, ignoring the envelope that Perry held out. "I need to talk to Serena alone."

Ryan pulled her along until he found a quiet spot, but Thom hovered nearby, watching them suspiciously.

"What deal?" Serena said.

"I told you about it," Ryan said. "Double my fee if I get you back to L.A., and triple if you marry Ben."

"But I thought you—"

"I'm not going to take it, Serena." He paused. "And I'm not going to stay in L.A. with you. I got you here, safe and sound, and now I'm going to leave you to sort out your life."

"No," Serena said. "You can't leave. I won't let you."

"Darling, I don't belong here."

"Neither do I. You made me see that. If you leave, I'm coming with you."

"No."

"You don't want me?"

"Of course I do," Ryan said. "I want you so much it aches inside. But you're the one who has to put this life behind you. You need to make the choice on your own." He drew her into his arms and kissed her, her body molding to his, her limbs limp with exhaustion.

Ryan drew away, smoothing his fingertips over her soft cheek. "I love you, Elly Sheridan. That is the only thing you need to remember. And when you are finished with this life, come back to me and we'll start *our* life together."

"And what if I'm not finished with this life?"

"I'll wait for you, for as long as it takes. There's no one else I'll love. You're the only one for me."

Ryan gently set her away from him, giving her shoulders a squeeze. "She's ready," he said to Thom Perry.

Thom slowly approached. Serena's gaze darted between the two of them, and for a moment, Ryan thought she was about to bolt. Then she took a ragged breath and closed her eyes, as if gathering her strength.

When she opened them again, she met his gaze. "I love you, too," she said. She walked over to Thom and took the envelope from his hand, then returned to Ryan. Rising up on her toes, Serena gently kissed his cheek. "See you later, Ryan," she murmured, pressing the envelope into his palm.

He held her hands for a long time, gazing into her

eyes, afraid to break the contact. But then she did, spinning to face Thom. "You, I barely tolerate," she muttered.

And with that, Serena Hightower walked away from him. Ryan watched her, hoping she'd turn back so he could get one last look at her. But she didn't. Serena was swallowed up by the crush of people on the concourse, and a minute later, it was as if she'd never existed at all, as if this whole romance had been a dream.

"I hope you didn't just make the biggest mistake of your life," he murmured to himself. He glanced around, searching for his bag, before realizing that Miles had taken it to the car. But then he saw the publicist, weaving his way through the crowd, Ryan's duffle thrown over his shoulder.

He rushed up and held out the bag. "You did the right thing," Miles said, breathless. "It never would have worked out between the two of you. Best to end it now."

And with that Miles left Ryan standing in the middle of the concourse, assaulted by self-doubt and regret. His only hope was that Serena was as strong as he thought she was. And that she truly did love him.

He picked up his bag and searched the signs for directions to the Air New Zealand ticket counter. When he found it, he got in line. He realized that he was still holding the envelope from Thom Perry.

Ryan tore it open and looked at the check. As promised, Thom had doubled his fee and added a substantial tip. Cursing softly, Ryan ripped the check into tiny bits, and when he reached the ticket clerk, he handed her the scraps.

"I'll need a ticket to Auckland," he said.

"When would you like to travel?" she asked, sending him a flirtatious smile.

"Now," Ryan said.

"We have a flight out at 10:15 tonight, nonstop. You'll be in Auckland the day after tomorrow at 7:15 a.m. Should I book that for you?"

"How much?" Ryan asked.

"Twelve hundred and eighty-one, U.S.," she said. "And how would you like to pay for that?"

Ryan pulled out his wallet and searched through his company bank cards, trying to find one that wasn't maxed out. Mal was going to kill him, especially if he found out that he'd ripped up a check that would have paid for ten tickets to Auckland.

Then, as the clerk ran his card through the reader, Ryan remembered that he was about to become a millionaire. Some distant relative, Aunt Aileen Quinn, had left him over a million dollars. He'd have enough money to live comfortably, to start his surf school.

But no amount of money could buy back the woman he loved if she decided not to return to New Zealand.

"MISS HIGHTOWER? DO YOU have a preference on this point?"

"What?" Serena moved her eyes away from the window and glanced around the group that had gathered in her Malibu beach house. "I don't care. Do what you think is best."

"Mr. Thayer won't agree to that," Adele Reston said. "Any statement that puts even a hint of the blame on him is something that we won't accept. Miss High-tower is the one who wants to cancel the wedding, not Mr. Thayer."

An argument broke out between her camp and Ben's, and Serena felt her irritation rise. She'd wanted to be a part of the discussion, but now that she was, she realized that she truly didn't care who said what about her. She just wanted out.

Her thoughts spun back to that moment in the airport. Even now she couldn't figure out why Ryan had left her.

He never ran from a challenge. The man climbed mountains for a living. He wouldn't be afraid to face a few angry publicists. So why throw her to the wolves?

There was something deeper at work here. Was this a test of her resolve? Serena took a ragged breath. These men and women weren't wolves, they were people, with problems to solve. And those problems had been caused by something she'd done.

"Stop!" she cried.

The room grew silent and she glanced around, all eyes fixed on her. She felt tears well in her eyes, but she refused to surrender. This was her life they were talking about, her mistakes and her regrets. She would control how they were handled.

"Here is what you'll release to the press," Serena began. "You'll say that Ben and I remain good friends and that we realized how difficult it would be to make a marriage work with our busy schedules. You'll say we still have the utmost respect for each other and wish each other the best."

The group nodded. "That sounds acceptable," Ben's publicist said. "And plausible."

"It's plausible because it's how I feel," Serena said softly. "And I hope it's how Ben feels, too."

"And this other man," Miles DuMont said. "What statement would you like us to release about him?"

Serena directed her attention to the studio publicist. "You won't mention him at all."

"They're going to want to know if you're together," Miles said.

Serena considered the question, a question she couldn't answer. Were they together? If they were, he'd be here at her side, trying to sort out this mess with her. She fought another wave of tears. He should be holding her hand and giving her advice and—

She drew a sharp breath, then turned away from the group, her gaze fixing on the horizon outside the wide glass windows again. No. Closing her eyes, she scolded herself silently. No! He'd been right to leave her. This was her life; these were her mistakes. Ryan had nothing to do with them, beyond providing a safe harbor in a storm when she'd needed it.

"If the subject of Mr. Quinn comes up, you will simply say that he was supportive during a very difficult time in my life and—"

"But they're going to want to know if—"

She spun around again. "You will not bring him into this. He had nothing to do with my decision to end the engagement or call off the wedding. That was entirely between me and Ben."

"They're going to want a reason," Adele, Ben's publicist insisted. "My client was blindsided and he will not—"

"Your client is not being entirely truthful with you," she said, turning her full attention on Adele. "If you want details, you can ask him. There are two rather... large details that I'm sure he'll be happy to provide." She saw the woman squirm in her seat and the color rise in her cheeks. "Or maybe three," Serena added. "But those are for him to reveal if he chooses, not for me."

Adele nodded nervously, and Serena decided to spare her any further distress and move on. "Next problem?"

"The wedding," Miles said. "The expense. Many of your fans are going to find the waste a bit difficult to rationalize. You were spending over a million on the ceremony and reception."

"Anything that was purchased, including my wedding dress, will be auctioned online and the proceeds will go to help the Los Angeles Humane Society. It's a charity both Ben and I support. Gifts will be returned. Vendors will be paid. My wedding planner will be taking care of those details. Any other questions on that subject?"

"The media tour for the movie," Miles said. "And the tour for the European release."

"I plan to fulfill all my commitments to the studio and abide by all my contract obligations. Since the wedding has been canceled, I will be available for appearances starting tomorrow."

Craig Zimmer, Serena's agent, raised his hand. "Don't you think it's a bit soon to—"

"No," Serena said. "I'm not an emotional wreck. I'm

choosing to look at these events as a positive step forward. I'm happy that I've been able to prevent Ben and I untold heartache later."

"Do you love him?"

Serena opened her mouth, ready to declare her feelings for Ryan, unafraid to say what she felt. But then she realized that the question had to do with Ben, not Ryan. "I will always love Ben," she said. "We've been very close for the past two years, and he is a dear friend. I know he'll find happiness." She forced a smile. "I think we've taken care of all the questions. This is nothing that can't be handled with the truth. I'm not trying to hide anything or spin the situation to my benefit. And I will be happy to answer further questions from the media."

"Are you sure it wouldn't be better to ask the media to respect your privacy?" Pauline Fredericks, Serena's publicist, asked.

"I can handle their questions, Pauline. The sooner they're addressed, the sooner the speculation will stop."

"Well, my client will be satisfied," Adele said. She snapped her notebook shut.

"There is one more subject that might come up," Miles said. "The studio's *Roman Holiday* remake has been green-lighted. Rumor is that Thom Perry wants you to reprise the Audrey Hepburn role. What's your position on that?"

A month ago, she'd have been thrilled to be considered for the role. She'd have actively sought it by making her interest clear to Miles and to the media. But Serena wasn't going to play the game anymore. "If I were offered the role, I'd consider it. But there's been no offer." She paused. "And in my opinion, Hollywood shouldn't tamper with perfection. There's no need to remake a classic."

This opinion clearly made Miles DuMont uneasy. Greenmoor Studios had been counting on her to help them sell the idea. She was the best choice for the role. No one else in Hollywood was right. But for the first time in forever, she'd said exactly what she thought. "If that's all, you can show yourselves out. I need to get my rest. I'm sure I'll have a lot of interviews tomorrow."

Serena stepped out onto the balcony and closed the door behind her. The sky had turned gray and she could smell rain in the air. Leaning against the rail, she drew a deep breath. She'd done it. She'd demanded the attention of all those people, and she'd made them listen and obey her wishes.

She heard the door open behind her, and a few seconds later, her agent, Craig Zimmer, stood beside her. "You did well," he said.

"Thanks," Serena replied.

"And you looked fabulous."

Serena laughed softly. "You don't have to stroke my ego, Craig. I really don't care how I look. All I want to do is crawl into bed and sleep."

"All right." He reached out and patted Serena's arm. "Is there anything I can do for you? Anything I can get you? Chicken soup? A massage therapist? A time machine?"

Serena shook her head. "No, I'll be fine. Nothing a bit of sleep won't cure."

"You made the right choice," Frank said.

"Did I?"

"Ben Thayer was not husband material. All your doubts were well-founded and then some. I'm so glad you figured him out in time."

"Why didn't you say something?"

"Because you wouldn't have listened. And it wasn't my place. I'm your agent."

"You're also my friend," Serena said.

"Then, as your friend, let me say that I think you're handling this extremely well. You might just come out of this unscathed if you play your cards right."

"I'm not going to be playing any cards. No more games. I'm going to do exactly what pleases me, and that's all. No more awards shows. I hate those things. The dresses and cameras and all the smiling and acting like it's wonderful. And I want you and Bill to work on getting me out of the contracts that I have. No more studio movies."

"But—"

"Independent films would be nice. Small roles. Two or three weeks of filming at most."

"Serena, I'm not sure—"

"It's what I want," Serena said. "If you have a problem with it, I can find another agent."

"You're going to ruin your career," he said.

Serena shrugged. "It wouldn't be the worst thing in the world."

"Serena, I know you're under a lot of stress. And you're tired. This will all look different in the morning, believe me. I'll call you tomorrow and we'll talk."

"I'm not going to change my mind," Serena said, pushing away from the rail. She walked back into the beach house and slowly climbed the stairs.

"We should discuss this," he called.

"Start working on those contracts," Serena said. "After everything hits the fan, I'm sure there are a few studios who'd be happy to dump me for another actress."

She meant what she said. From now on, she was going to do only what made her happy. She wasn't going to play the game. And if that wasn't enough, then she'd accept the consequences. Serena loved to act. She just didn't like being a movie star. If there was a way to separate the actress from the movie star, then she was determined to find it.

When she got to her room, she flopped down onto her bed, burying her face in a thick down pillow. She'd sorted out her professional life, but it was going to take a lot more energy to figure out her personal life.

"DANA, ARE THESE really necessary? Can't you just leave them at home?" Ryan picked up the magazine and stared at the photo of Serena, ignoring the sensational headline.

The woman on the cover didn't look like the Serena he'd fallen in love with. This was the Hollywood Serena, not the beauty who'd warmed his bed and made his body ache with desire. No one knew that Serena—except him.

It had been six weeks since he'd left her at the airport. For the first couple of days, he'd understood when she hadn't called because she was busy with the publicity tour. And it was the holiday season. After that, he'd left for Kilimanjaro and then the Alps, and communication was difficult, not that she'd tried. But there were no excuses now.

"Call her," Dana said, snatching the magazine from his hand.

"Why are you so sure that I haven't?"

"Oh, please. If you'd been talking to her, you wouldn't look like some sad puppy dog, drooling over her pictures and staring off into the distance. You love her. She loves you. Why make it so complicated?" She sighed and handed him an envelope. "This should make you happy."

"What is it?"

"It's from our aunt Aileen."

He opened the envelope and withdrew the check. "Wow. That's a big check."

"I know! When I saw mine, I just sat there for ten minutes, staring at it. It's hard to believe it's real."

"It's not real," he murmured. "It's lucky money."

"Of course it's lucky. Lucky Aunt Aileen found us." She snatched the envelope away from him. "If you don't want it, I'll take it."

Ryan had struggled with his pride when it came to money. It had bothered him that Serena made a lot more money than he did and always would. Now, living without her, Ryan realized how stupid he'd been.

Money had nothing to do with his feelings for her. He didn't love her any more or any less because of what she made—or what he didn't make. Aileen had given all her money away to make her heirs happy. And all she'd asked for in exchange was a visit and a few hours of his time.

A million dollars. He could buy the surf school. He could build a life for them. But she didn't want that life anymore. "I have a suggestion," Dana said. "Why don't you take some of that money, buy a ticket and go visit Aunt Aileen. And then stop by England on your way home and see Serena."

"I'm not even sure she's there," Ryan said.

"She's there," Dana said.

"How do you know?"

"She sent me a gift. The return address was her place in England."

"Why would she send you a gift?"

"It was just something silly. A nail polish that she liked and wanted me to try. The perfect shade of pink." Dana paused. "I could give you the address."

"Yes. All right," he murmured. "Wait. No."

"Ryan, if you want her, you're going to have to let her know."

"It's not that simple. She needs to decide what she wants first. If she decides to keep making movies, how is that going to work?"

"So, you leave on expeditions from Los Angeles or London. Rogan works out of Sydney. We could use a Los Angeles office. It might help business."

"That's not the problem. It's when, not where. When are we going to be together? Even if I leave Max Adrenaline and do my own thing, I know how hard it is to make a relationship work when one person is gone for weeks at a time."

"If you're really in love, you'd make it work."

If. If he was in love, then all of these decisions would be simple. He'd want to be with her, no matter where they were. He'd be willing to give up everything to follow her around the world. He'd happily become Mr. Hightower.

"I have to get out of here," he muttered. "Where's Duffy? I'm taking him home."

"Sleeping with a dog is not going to replace sleeping with the woman you love," Dana said.

"Give it a rest," he said.

He found Duffy asleep on the porch. He called to the dog, and Duffy leaped to his feet and trotted after him. He opened the door of the Range Rover, and Duffy jumped inside. Ryan got behind the wheel, then sat back in the seat and stared out the windscreen.

He started the car and pulled out of the car park. As long as they loved each other, they could make it work. But how many couples made that promise, then later got divorced? Marriage was difficult under the best circumstances, and he and Serena were starting with the worst. Look what had happened to his own parents.

As he drove through Raglan, he wondered if maybe he shouldn't have forced her to go back. Maybe he should have just gone along with what she wanted, to stay with him and forget her old life entirely. If he hadn't pushed her, she'd be here with him now, planning their future. He realized then that's what he wanted more than anything else—a future with Serena, no matter what it took.

He and Serena weren't his parents. Ryan wasn't his

father, and he wouldn't make the same mistakes. He kept his promises.

"You've managed to make a mess out of this," he muttered. "Now how are you going to fix it?"

He'd start by buying a ticket to England. He'd give her a month. The scandal of her canceled wedding was starting to fade and she ought to know how she really felt about him. He'd do whatever it took to be with her.

As he finished the drive home, Ryan thought about what he'd say to Serena. He had to offer her a plan, a way to make their lives mesh. It wasn't enough to tell her that he loved her, was it?

When he pulled the car into the drive of the *bach*, he noticed a Toyota SUV parked in his spot. He frowned, wondering which of his brothers had bought a new truck. Obviously one of them had started spending their money.

Duffy trotted next to him. When he reached for the screen door, Ryan heard barking coming from behind the house. Duffy's ears pricked up and he took off around the corner of the cottage. Curious, Ryan followed him, striding down the narrow path to the beach. When he got to the sand, he found a group of dogs racing around along the water's edge.

Duffy had already joined in the play, chasing a small terrier back and forth along the beach. A larger dog came trotting up to him and nuzzled his hand. Ryan bent down and patted his head. "What's your name, mate?"

"His name is Riley."

The sound of her voice sent a tremor through his body. Ryan slowly stood, then turned to find Serena standing behind him. She wore a pretty blue dress that clung to her slender form. Her face was scrubbed clean of makeup, and her hair was a different color than he remembered.

"Are these all yours?" he asked.

Serena nodded. "I figured if we just moved in, you couldn't say no."

"You think I don't want you here?" He crossed the distance between them and pulled her body against his, his lips coming down on hers in a long, deep kiss. "I was coming to you. I love you. I want you wherever and whenever you call."

She laughed, then kissed him again. "I've missed you so much. You were right. I needed to go back. And once I sorted everything out, my life was suddenly so much clearer. I know exactly what I want now."

"Please say it includes me," Ryan murmured, smoothing his hands over her pretty face.

"Of course it does. I have a plan." She took his hand and led him back into the house, calling for the dogs to follow her. When they got inside, the dogs, including Duffy, settled down and began to jockey for spots on the sofa and chairs.

Ryan and Serena watched them in amusement. "One big happy family," he said.

"This is what I wanted to show you," she said. She crossed to the kitchen island and picked up a giant calendar. As he paged through it, he noticed some weeks crossed out. "If we work hard at it, we can do this. I've decided to cut down to two films a year and those will be indie films. So maybe two months of work. The rest of the time, I'll live here. Is that acceptable?"

"Are we negotiating?"

"Now you have to make your offer. Then we negotiate," she said.

"All right. I'm going to buy the surf school. Every now and then, I want to help my brothers by guiding a trip, but it will be no more than two a year. Is that acceptable?"

"We'll travel with each other as much as possible," she said.

"And we'll take time for ourselves, to plan our own vacations."

She nodded. "Those terms are acceptable to me."

"They're acceptable to me, too," Ryan said. "So, do we need to put this in writing or will a kiss seal our promise?"

"A kiss would work," she said.

"Is this going to be a real kiss or a show-biz kiss?"

"Oh, it will be very real." Serena caught his bottom lip between her teeth, then gave him the most seductive kiss he'd ever experienced, leaving him breathless with desire.

"Have you missed me?" she asked.

"Not at all."

Serena stepped back and gave him a dubious look. "Not at all?"

"I've been enjoying your company every night," he said. Ryan walked over to the bookshelf and removed a large stack of DVDs. "I bought them all. Even the one where you get eaten by a zombie in the first ten minutes."

"You watched all of my films?"

"I have. I can speak with authority now." He tossed the DVDs on the sofa and slipped his arms around her waist again. "You are an incredible actress. And I think you should keep doing what you love to do."

"Even if I make a lot of money at it?"

Ryan nodded. "I'm working on my issues with that. It doesn't feel quite right now, but if you give me some time, I'll come around. Besides, I've now got a bit of money of my own." He explained about his newfound relative, Aileen Quinn, and his family's windfall. He paused. "By the way, the new bed came right before the holiday. And it's a little large for just me. You want to try it out?"

She nodded and pulled him toward the bedroom. But he stopped her. "There is one more point I need to discuss. And this is very important." Ryan took her hand and stared down into her eyes. "When the time is right, I'm going to ask you to marry me. You're going to say yes, and we're going to have a simple wedding, maybe on the beach, with our friends and family there. And we're going to have a few kids and enjoy our life together. And we're going to live well past one hundred and love each other forever. Is that acceptable to you?"

Serena smiled, tears swimming in her eyes. "Yes," she said. "It is. All of it."

Ryan grabbed her around the waist and hugged her, picking her up off her feet. The dogs started barking and he glanced around at the chaos. "How did you get all these dogs here?"

"I chartered a jet."

"A jet?" He put her back on her feet. "You chartered a jet to bring your dogs to New Zealand?"

"Yes. We had to land twice for potty breaks, but it wasn't so bad."

Ryan chuckled softly and pulled her into his embrace. "You're an amazing woman, Elly Sheridan. And I'm glad you decided to come home."

THE PARTY WAS in full swing when Serena and Ryan arrived. Many of the three-thousand-plus residents of Raglan had stopped by to wish the Quinn brothers good luck on their expedition to Mount Everest. They'd signed a huge banner and strung it up on the wall, a banner that would travel to the Himalayas and hang in the base-camp communications tent.

Over the past couple of months, Serena had met many of the residents around town, and though she'd at first been a bit of a curiosity, it wasn't long before they forgot about her celebrity and treated her like any other citizen.

As she walked through the crowd, her new friends greeted her with smiles and hugs. She'd gone her whole life without real friends, and now she had a town full of them. And a family, too.

Ryan's family had accepted her into their midst without hesitation. And in addition to Ryan's brothers, she now had sisters in Dana, Amy and Claudia. They didn't see her as a celebrity. They saw her as the woman Ryan loved, and that was enough for them.

Amy spotted her and came over to give her a hug. "How are you doing?"

"I'm scared," she said. "I don't want him to go."

"Oh, I know."

"They'll be gone for two months. It seems like forever. We haven't been together that long."

"Dana is bringing good communication equipment. You should be able to talk to him almost every night. Either on the phone or with a video chat."

"It's still going to be difficult. But I'm leaving in a couple of weeks for a shoot. Maybe that will make the time go faster."

Claudia came up a few moments later and also gave her a hug. "How are you doing?"

Amy giggled. "I just asked her that. She's says she fine, but she really isn't. Maybe I should get you a drink, Serena."

"No, I'm fine. Really," Serena said. "I could use some cake, though. I've been trying to take off my New Zealand fifteen, but I don't care tonight."

Serena found a table and sat down to enjoy her cake, taking in the people around her, husbands and wives, children. She'd found the perfect place to begin her new life. Looking back, it had been a long and twisted road. But everything that had happened had led her to this moment, to the realization that she finally had what she wanted.

She had Ryan and their little *bach* on the beach, her dogs, a bed big enough for all of them. And she also had her career—on her terms. She would make it work, traveling between her two lives. But her heart would always remain with Ryan.

She drew a ragged breath, fighting back the tears. There wasn't a moment she regretted her choice. And with every day they spent together, she loved Ryan more than the previous day.

"Ladies and gentlemen, may I have your attention. Gather around." Mal stood on a small platform at the far end of the hall. A cameraman was filming the event for a documentary that would follow the expedition. For once, Serena was glad the cameras weren't turned on her.

"I want to thank you all for coming to wish us well on our trip to Everest." Mal paused. "Not many of you knew my father, so I'd like to tell you a little bit about him."

Over the next ten minutes, Mal paid tribute to Max Quinn, explaining what it had been like to grow up with a man who risked his life to conquer the world's highest peaks, how it hadn't been easy to grow up in that shadow, but now he felt his father would be proud of him. Lydie stood beside Mal, tears swimming in her eyes as she remembered her husband, alive and well.

Mal went on to thank the sponsors of the expedition and then said a few words about Amy and how much he loved her. He called Amy up on stage and handed her an enormous bouquet of flowers.

Rogan was next and he added a few remarks, touching on his own journey to find peace with his father's memory. He had another list of thanks and then jumped off the platform to sweep Claudia into a dramatic kiss. The guests broke out in a rousing round of applause, shouting and whistling for the two of them.

Ryan was next. He wasn't much for public speaking, but he grabbed the microphone and took center stage. "Hello, everyone. Thanks for coming tonight. As you all know, we're leaving tomorrow morning to complete a journey that our father began almost twenty years ago. I wasn't always an advocate for this trip, but I've had several moments of clarity over the past few months, and I appreciate now how important this is to my family. So, thank you Mal and Rogan and Dana for helping me see the importance of this expedition. I've come to understand my father better in the last couple of months, and I've also come to forgive him. I realize now that you can let someone go without having to lose them, because they will always be in your heart."

The audience clapped and he moved to step off the stage, but then turned back. "There's one more thing. I'd like to thank my darling Serena, for all of her love and support. I was going to do this later tonight, but I don't want to wait. Serena, where are you? Come on up here."

The audience clapped again and they searched the room for her. Reluctantly, she approached the stage and Ryan held out his hand, helping her onto the platform.

"What's this about?"

"Just wait," he said.

A moment later he was down on one knee. Serena stared at him for a long moment, trying to figure out what was going on. But then he pulled a small box out of his pocket. "Before I leave, I have an important question to ask. I promised you this would come, and I think it's time. Are you ready?"

The guests shouted their approval and Ryan laughed, looking up at Serena for her decision. "I'm ready," she said.

"Ellsbeth Serena Hightower Sheridan, will you do me the very great honor of agreeing to become my wife?"

Serena stared down at him, her eyes flooded with tears. This was the way a proposal was meant to be, she thought to herself. She was filled with so much love, and it felt as though she might burst from pure happiness. She wasn't afraid or confused; she was absolutely certain that Ryan was the man for her.

"Well?" he asked.

"Yes, I will marry you, Ryan."

He stood up and pulled her into a fierce hug. "You don't have to be afraid, Serena. I'll love you forever."

"I love you, too," she said.

He pulled the ring out of the box and placed it on her finger. It wasn't a huge, flashy diamond. Instead, he'd chosen an antique ruby in a platinum setting. It was the most beautiful ring she'd ever seen. But it wasn't the ring that made the difference. She'd found a man who loved her for the woman she was, a man who helped her to be a better person.

The band began to play, and Ryan took her hand and led her out to the dance floor. But he didn't stop there. Instead, he walked through the crowd to the front door.

"Where are we going?" she asked.

"Home," he said. "I can't kiss you the way I want to kiss you in the middle of this crowd."

"You have the rest of your life to kiss me," she said.

"Yes, but I'm going to be living in a tent at the top of the world in a few more weeks. I'm going to need some memories to take with me."

"So you're going all the way to the top? You're not staying at base camp?"

"I'm ready to face whatever's up there because I know you're down here waiting for me."

Serena laughed, then wrapped her arms around his neck. "Then take me home," she said.

It was a powerful word—home. It meant so many things to so many people. But for Serena it was the end of a long and winding road. She'd found what she'd been searching for and nothing, not even a mountain, would stand between them.

Epilogue

THE PHOTO OF the three Quinn brothers on the summit of Everest was posted on the company website the day after they made it safely back to base camp. Aileen Quinn stared at the three young men, bundled from head to toe in cold-weather gear, and felt a sense of pride at their accomplishment.

But it was tempered with sadness when her gaze fell on the photos of Max Quinn's final resting place. Sherpas had covered the body with rocks they'd gathered from the area and the boys had each read a poem over their father's grave before continuing their descent.

Aileen couldn't imagine how difficult it must have been to relive the tragedy of their father's death. But they'd retrieved Max's journal and were able to read the words their father had written in his last hours. They'd posted excerpts on their website.

"'I can't go on,'" Aileen read softly. "'My ankle is broken, and it won't support my weight. If I don't make it through the night and rescue is impossible, please know that I did my best to come home to you, my darlings. I send you all my love and bid you to look to the sky every now and then. I'll be there, in the stars and the sun, the clouds and the rain. I will keep you safe.'" She drew a slow breath. "Oh, poor Maxwell."

"Aileen?"

She looked up to find Ian Stephens standing in the doorway of her office. "Am I disturbing you?"

"No, of course not," Aileen said. "Come, come," she said, motioning to him. "I'm just reading about my nephews' little jaunt to the top of the world's highest mountain. It's quite exciting."

"I've seen the photos. Claire has been caught up in the adventure, too. Did you see the one of Dana?"

"No," Aileen said.

Ian stood over her shoulder and helped her scroll through the row of thumbnails. "Here it is."

She clicked on one and a photo popped up of Dana, a silly grin on her pretty face. She was wrapped in her sleeping bag and reading a book. "Is that my—oh, goodness! She's reading an Aileen Quinn book."

"Even on the top of the world you have fans," Ian said.

They looked through the remainder of the photos, talking about the adventure. And when they were finished, Aileen sat back and sighed. "I'm almost sad it's over."

"The climb? I'd expect you'd be happy they were safe."

"No, I was talking about our search." She got to her feet and slowly walked to the window, fighting back a wave of emotion. Outside the Irish country house, a cold rain drizzled down the leaded glass and the April sky was gray and dreary.

She'd learned over the years to appreciate all of the seasons. Though it marked the passing of time, she was grateful to see the changes. Grateful to be alive.

She turned and faced Ian. "It's been fun, hasn't it?"

"It has. And who can say, we may discover a few more Quinns that we didn't know existed."

"I'm not sure I could take many more. I'm running out of money to give them." She saw the expression on Ian's face, then waved her hand. "Oh, don't worry. I was only teasing you. I have more than enough to be comfortable for the rest of my life, however long that is."

"I hope it's very long," Ian said. "Now that we've come to be friends and I've married into the family, I want you to stick around. We need our family matriarch."

"I can't guarantee you anything," Aileen said. "At ninety-eight, I'm just happy to be able to get out of bed every day."

"You're a treasure, Aileen. Look at what you've done for your brothers. They would have been proud to call you sister."

"I would have given my entire fortune to have known them. I think about that a lot these days. I wonder if I'll meet them on the other side, if we'll have a chance to be a real family."

Ian stood up and crossed the room to stand by Aileen's side. He took her hand and slipped it into the crook of his elbow. "Claire's laid tea in the sitting room. Let's go in and have a cup. We have some news for you."

Aileen smiled to herself as she walked through the house. It wasn't difficult to predict what they were about to tell her. She could see it in Claire's appearance, in the glow of her skin and the thickening of her waist. She was about to welcome another Quinn heir into her world.

And the journey would continue, even after she was gone. But for as long as she was here, she'd enjoy every Quinn she was blessed to meet.

* * * * *

Don't miss Kate Hoffmann's next book,
SEDUCING THE MARINE,
available January 2015!

COMING NEXT MONTH FROM

Available November 18, 2014

#823 A LAST CHANCE CHRISTMAS

Sons of Chance

by Vicki Lewis Thompson

Snowbound at the Last Chance Ranch, genealogist Molly Gallagher discovers just how talented custom saddle maker Ben Radcliffe is—in the bedroom and out! But is their scorching attraction enough to keep them together for more than one hot night?

#824 BRING ME TO LIFE

Uniformly Hot!

by Kira Sinclair

The military told Tatum Huntley her Special Ops husband was dead, so when he turns up three years later she can't decide if she should kill him herself or kiss him senseless!

#825 WILD HOLIDAY NIGHTS

3 stories in 1!

by Samantha Hunter, Meg Maguire and Debbi Rawlins

Three steamy Christmas stories. Three drop-dead gorgeous heroes. Three heroines finding out just how wild their nights can get when they're *not* home for the holidays!

#826 UNDER THE MISTLETOE

Holiday Heat

by Katherine Garbera

Penny's thrilled to meet a hot guy to share the holiday with. Gorgeous Will Spalding may just be the best gift she ever got! But can she walk away from the man of her dreams after two weeks together?

REQUEST YOUR FREE BOOKS!
2 FREE NOVELS PLUS 2 FREE GIFTS!

HARLEQUIN®
Blaze®

red-hot reads!

YES! Please send me 2 FREE Harlequin® Blaze™ novels and my 2 FREE gifts (gifts are worth about \$10). After receiving them, if I don't wish to receive any more books, I can return the shipping statement marked "cancel." If I don't cancel, I will receive 4 brand-new novels every month and be billed just \$4.74 per book in the U.S. or \$4.96 per book in Canada. That's a savings of at least 14% off the cover price. It's quite a bargain. Shipping and handling is just 50¢ per book in the U.S. and 75¢ per book in Canada.* I understand that accepting the 2 free books and gifts places me under no obligation to buy anything. I can always return a shipment and cancel at any time. Even if I never buy another book, the two free books and gifts are mine to keep forever.

150/350 HDN F4WC

Name _____ (PLEASE PRINT)

Address _____ Apt. #

City _____ State/Prov. _____ Zip/Postal Code

Signature (if under 18, a parent or guardian must sign)

Mail to the **Harlequin® Reader Service:**
IN U.S.A.: P.O. Box 1867, Buffalo, NY 14240-1867
IN CANADA: P.O. Box 609, Fort Erie, Ontario L2A 5X3

Want to try two free books from another line?
Call 1-800-873-8635 or visit www.ReaderService.com.

* Terms and prices subject to change without notice. Prices do not include applicable taxes. Sales tax applicable in N.Y. Canadian residents will be charged applicable taxes. Offer not valid in Quebec. This offer is limited to one order per household. Not valid for current subscribers to Harlequin Blaze books. All orders subject to credit approval. Credit or debit balances in a customer's account(s) may be offset by any other outstanding balance owed by or to the customer. Please allow 4 to 6 weeks for delivery. Offer available while quantities last.

Your Privacy—The Harlequin® Reader Service is committed to protecting your privacy. Our Privacy Policy is available online at www.ReaderService.com or upon request from the Harlequin Reader Service.

We make a portion of our mailing list available to reputable third parties that offer products we believe may interest you. If you prefer that we not exchange your name with third parties, or if you wish to clarify or modify your communication preferences, please visit us at www.ReaderService.com/consumerschoice or write to us at Harlequin Reader Service Preference Service, P.O. Box 9062, Buffalo, NY 14269. Include your complete name and address.

HB13R2

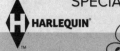 
New York Times bestselling author
Vicki Lewis Thompson is back with another
irresistible story from her bestselling
miniseries *Sons of Chance!*

A Last Chance Christmas

She stood on tiptoe, wound her arms around his neck and gave it all she had. So did he, and oh, my goodness. A harmonica player knew what it was all about. She'd never kissed one before, but she hoped to be doing a lot more of this with Ben.

Although she'd never thought of a kiss as being creative, this one was. He caressed her lips so well and so thoroughly that she forgot the cold and the late hour. She forgot they were standing in a cavernous tractor barn surrounded by heavy equipment.

She even forgot that she wasn't in the habit of kissing men she'd known for mere hours. Come to think of it, she'd never done that. But everything about this kiss, from his dessert-flavored taste to his talented tongue, felt perfect.

As far as she was concerned, the kiss could go on forever. Well, maybe not. The longer they kissed, the heavier they breathed. His hot mouth was making her light-headed in more ways than one.

That was her excuse for dropping her phone on the concrete floor. It hit with a sickening crack, but in her current aroused state, she didn't really care.

Ben pulled back, though, and gulped for air. "I think that was your phone."

"I think so, too." She dragged in a couple of quick breaths. "Kiss me some more."

With a soft groan, he lowered his head and settled his mouth over hers. This time he took the kiss deeper and invested it with a meaning she understood quite well. Intellectually she was shocked, but physically she was completely on board.

This time when he eased away from her, she was trembling. Like a swimmer breaking the surface, she gasped. Then she clutched his head and urged him back down. She wanted him to kiss her until her conscience stopped yelling at her that it was too soon to feel like this about him. "More."

**Pick up A LAST CHANCE CHRISTMAS
by Vicki Lewis Thompson,
on sale December 2014,
wherever Harlequin® Blaze® books are sold.**

When it snows, things get really steamy...

Wild Holiday Nights

from Harlequin Blaze offers something sweet, something unexpected and something naughty!

Holiday Rush by *Samantha Hunter*

Cake guru Calla Michaels is canceling Christmas to deal with fondant, batter and an attempted robbery. Then Gideon Stone shows up at her door. Apparently, Calla's kitchen isn't hot enough without having her longtime crush in her bakery...*and* in her bed!

Playing Games by *Meg Maguire*

When her plane is grounded on Christmas eve, Carrie Baxter is desperate enough to share a rental car with her secret high-school crush. Sure, Daniel Barber is much, *much* hotter, but he's still just as prickly as ever. It's gonna be one *looong* drive...and an unforgettably X-rated night!

All Night Long by *Debbi Rawlins*

The only way overworked paralegal Carly Watts gets her Christmas vacation is by flying to Chicago to get Jack Carrington's signature. But Jack's in no rush to sell his grandfather's company. In fact, he'll do whatever it takes to buy more time. Even if it takes one naughty night before Christmas...

Available December 2014 wherever you buy
Harlequin Blaze books.

HARLEQUIN®

Blaze

Red-Hot Reads

www.Harlequin.com

Love the Harlequin book you just read?

Your opinion matters.

Review this book on your favorite book site, review site, blog or your own social media properties and share your opinion with other readers!